Thomas Wagstaffe

Piety Promoted

Thomas Wagstaffe

Piety Promoted

ISBN/EAN: 9783337400750

Printed in Europe, USA, Canada, Australia, Japan

Cover: Foto ©Andreas Hilbeck / pixelio.de

More available books at **www.hansebooks.com**

PIETY PROMOTED,

IN

BRIEF MEMORIALS

OF THE

VIRTUOUS LIVES,

SERVICES,

AND

DYING SAYINGS,

Of feveral of the

PEOPLE called QUAKERS.

THE EIGHTH PART.

By THOMAS WAGSTAFFE.

Light is fown for the Righteous, and Gladnefs for the
Upright in Heart, Pfal. xcvii. 11.
The Righteous hath Hope in his Death, Prov. xiv. 32.

LONDON:

Printed and Sold by MARY HINDE, at
Nº 2, in George-Yard, Lombard-Street.

M DCC LXXIV.

THE
PREFACE
TO THE
READER.

THE Memorials of the Perfons, mentioned in this Work, were extracted from Teftimonies concerning them, or other authentic Accounts, and are collected, as thofe in the feven preceding Volumes were, with a View to the Promotion of Piety and Virtue ; that by having the Footfteps of thofe before them, who have finifhed their Courfe well, others might be excited and encouraged to follow them as they followed Chrift.

The PREFACE.

It is in my Heart more particularly to addreſs the riſing Youth, with De-ſires that they may be raiſed up and qualified to fill the Places of thoſe who are gone from Works to Rewards ; that the Teſtimony given us to bear may be faithfully maintained, the Borders of Sion enlarged, and the glorious un-changeable Truth, in the Courſe of Divine Wiſdom, be more eſtabliſhed among Men.

And firſt, to thoſe of both Sexes, who are yet in their Minority, and who often feel the Touches of Divine Love tendering their Hearts, and draw-ing them to Good and the Love of good Men, tho' perhaps (like *Samuel* when a Child) they may at firſt be ignorant of the Cauſe thereof : Let theſe therefore be intreated not to get from under theſe precious Viſitations, but as they feel them to ariſe, be careful not to neglect, much leſs oppoſe them ;

and

and in due Time fuch will experience
them to be a Degree of that Divine
Light, *which lighteth every Man that*
cometh into the World, John i. 9. By
bringing all their Thoughts, Words
and Actions thereto, they will clearly
difcern the Ground and Tendency of
them.

It was through the Influence of this
Divine Principle, many were led in
very early Youth to wait for and feek
after that Confolation which they had
felt, without knowing from whence it
came, until he who firft vifited, enlarged their Underftandings, and led
them to a further Degree of Knowledge, and convinced them it was of a
Divine Nature, and that their Growth
in true Virtue lay in a fteady Attention
thereto.

To thofe who are of riper Years, and
who have been mercifully favour'd with
a further

a further Enlargement of this Divine Life, and are in meafure turned to it; the Safety of all fuch depends in waiting for its Inftructions, and under its Heavenly Influence faithfully following them. Let thefe be encouraged in the Language of the Prophet: *Then fhall we know, if we follow on to know the Lord, his Going forth is prepared as the Morning; and he fhall come unto us as the Rain, as the latter and former Rain unto the Earth,* Hofea vi. 3.

Thefe will, in true Wifdom, fee the Service of their Day, feel Divine Support through this State of Probation, and Prefervation to the End; partaking as they go along of that Peace which Chrift promifed his true Followers, *Peace I leave with you, my Peace I give unto you, not as the World giveth, give I unto you,* John xiv. 27.

It

It was this which supported the Righteous in all Ages, and is Cause of Encouragement to look forwards ; the same Hand which supported our Predecessors, is still near to help us in every needful Time. Thus by filling up every Duty, we may experience in our Conclusion, the Truth of the Prophet's Declaration, that *The Work of Righteousness shall be Peace, and the Effect of Righteousness, Quietness and Assurance for ever*, Isaiah xxxii. 17.

T. W.

London, the 8th of the
Firrt Month 1774.

PIETY

PIETY PROMOTED.

THE EIGHTH PART.

SAMUEL CATER, formerly of *Littleport* in the Ifle of *Ely*, was convinced of the Principles of Truth, as held by the People called *Quakers*, about the Year 1655, by the Miniſtry of *James Parnel*, who (though but a Youth about eighteen Years of Age) was raiſed up powerfully to preach the Goſpel, and became inſtrumental in the ſettling and eſtabliſhing many therein, both by Teſtimony and Writing, and finiſhed his Courſe in *Colcheſter* Caſtle before he reached his twentieth Year, for his Teſtimony to the Truth ; for a further Account of whom, ſee Vol. I. Page the 1ſt. of *Piety Promoted*, and a Collection of his own Writings.

Soon after his Convincement, the ſaid *Samuel Cater* was excommunicated by the

B   *Baptiſts*,

Baptists, among whom he had walked ; and by the Records of Friends Sufferings it appears he was divers Times imprisoned for his Testimony to the Truth : With respect to his *Christian* Progress through a long Course of Years from his Convincement to his Decease, no particular Account appears, but what is noted above.

About the Latter-end of the Seventh Month 1711, he was taken ill ; in the Course of which Illness he express'd himself to some Friends and Neighbours who came to visit him to this Effect : *That God would have them to be saved,* and desired them to *mind the Grace of God that bringeth Salvation, or the Light of Jesus Christ in their Consciences that reproveth for Evil,* which he often repeated, with many more such like Expressions to all that came to see him in his last Illness, desiring them that were not of our Society, *not to take it ill that he spoke to them, for it was in true Love to their Souls, and that they might not put off Time till Strength failed, for they would find enough to do to wrestle with the Pains of the Body ;* therefore, says he, *prize your Time.* At another Time when in great Pain, he desired, *That he might quietly hope, and patiently wait for the Salvation of God ; for neither Grace nor Glory, nor any good Thing would the Lord withhold from them that walk*

walk uprightly. Often praising God *that he felt the Presence of his dear Son Jesus Christ, who died on the Cross for all, to fill his Soul.* Again desiring, *that he and his House might serve the Lord, let others do as they would ;* and remarked, that *Caleb* said, *He was Four-score and five Years of Age, and he was as strong for War as he was forty Years before : I am,* says he, *going of Four-score and six, and I am as strong for the spiritual War as I was forty Years ago.*

To his Daughter *Elizabeth Hawkes,* he would say with great Zeal on First and Fourth Days, being Meeting Days ; *Come, dear Child, let us wait on the Lord, that though we be absent in Body, we may not be in Spirit.* Often speaking very comfortably to his Wife and Daughter, saying, *He felt little Pain, but a Difficulty of Breathing ; and that he was well satisfied with the Will of the Lord. If he lived, he hoped to live to the Lord ; and if it was his Lot to die, he felt true Satisfaction therein, and it would be Gain to him to be in his Father's Kingdom, to behold the Glory of his Reedeemer Jesus Christ.*

A Friend taking Leave of him, he said, *Dear Child, the Lord be with thee and many more. Mind, it's an excellent Blessing to feel and witness the Ancient of Days to be with his*

B 2   *People,*

People, without whose Presence we are poor nothing Creatures, and not of ourselves able to do any thing to the Honour of our God. Not long before his Departure, his Eyes being shut, he felt for his Daughter's Hand, and said, *Dear Child, I find the Man's Words fulfilled.* She asking what Man? He answered, *The first* Quaker *that I saw: I was at Work upon such a House in the Town; he looked upon me, and bad me Repent, for the Kingdom of Heaven was at hand: And now I can say it is at hand. Magnified be thy holy Name, O Lord!* Several Times expressing *he felt the Kingdom nigh his Soul.* The Day before he died, he said, *Now, O Lord! doth my Eyes see thy Salvation, now let thy Servant depart in Peace.* Being much pent for Breath, he said, *Lord, thou that gavest me Breath, canst take it away, if it be thy Will, do so: Not my Will but thine be done, O Lord my God!*

He departed this Life the 19th of the Eighth Month 1711. Aged near eighty-six Years.

GILBERT THOMPSON, of Sankey in *Lancashire*, was born at *Sedburg* in *Yorkshire*, about the Year 1658. He was in his Time a Man of great Use and Service in the Church, and in his Station of a School-master was eminently qualified for the Instruction of Youth, being endued with Wisdom and Skill to govern them by mild and gentle Means, labouring to find out their several Dispositions that his Application might be suitable thereto ; and being an Example of Humility and good Conversation, his Labours for their Instruction was manifest in their Improvement in Learning, Understanding and Conduct : And while under his Care, many of them were so reached by Truth, and made like tender Plants replenished with Heavenly Dew, as gave Encouragement to hope they might prove useful in due Season, which has been verified since in divers.

But as it's common when Truth prevails, the Enemies thereof stir up War ; so by some envious Persons this our Friend was persecuted for keeping a School, and carried Prisoner to *Lancaster* Castle, which he bore

bore with *Christian* Patience, till difcharged by due Courfe of Law.

About the forty-firft Year of his Age, he was called to the Miniftry, in which his Labours were edifying, being pure and unmixed with enticing Words of Man's Wifdom. He travelled through moft Parts of *Great-Britain* and *Ireland*, where his Service was well accepted, his whole Converfation chearful, yet innocent, was agreeable to the Gofpel. As if fenfible of his approaching Conclufion, he vifited his Friends in his native Country, and at *London*, and fignified his great Satisfaction therein, faying, *His Time drew near for his being divefted of his earthly Tabernacle* ; which proved fo, for about two Weeks after his Return Home, he was feized with an *intermitting Fever*, and in about two Weeks more died, bearing his Sicknefs with Patience, faying, *He had done his Day's Work.*

He died the 22d of the Fourth Month 1719, at his Houfe at *Sankey*, and was buried the 25th of the fame at *Penketh*. Aged fixty-one Years.

JOHN

JOHN BUTCHER, of the City of *London*, was born of religious Parents, in the Seventh Month 1666, about two Weeks after the dreadful Conflagration ; his Father lived to a great Age, dying about his eighty-eighth Year, and his Mother about her fixty eighth Year ; both leaving a fweet Memorial behind them.

He, the faid *John*, was by them religioufly educated in the Way of Truth, and through the Grace of God, early receiving it in the Love thereof, it pleafed the Lord to endue him with a Degree of the Gofpel Miniftry, and to open his Mouth about the fifteenth Year of his Age, in a publick Teftimony to the true Light Chrift Jefus, not only in his outward, but alfo, and more efpecially, in his inward Appearance by his Grace and Holy Spirit ; and he gradually grew therein, and became an able Minifter, not of the Letter, but of the Spirit.

He travelled into divers Parts of this Nation, being well accepted therein, labouring for the Profperity of Truth, a Lover of Peace, Unity and Concord ; and being endued with a large Portion of Wifdom and
Underftanding

Underftanding in the Things of God, was enabled to fpeak to the States and Conditions of many. He was a Peace-maker, endeavouring to heal Breaches and reconcile Differences among Brethren.

He retained unfeigned Love to his Brethren to the End of his Days, altho' afflicted with great Weaknefs for fome Time before his Death, which impaired his Memory ; yet that true Love continued in him, was evident by his chearful Countenance, friendly and courteous Deportment. In a Vifit of fome Friends about a Year before his Deceafe, he expreffed himfelf very fenfibly, with refpect to the Lord's tender Dealings with him all along, and the Hope he had of Happinefs through Chrift.

George *Whitehead* and Gilbert *Molleson* vifiting him, he expreffed his kind Acceptance thereof, and took it as a Token of the Love and Mercy of God to him ; and fignify'd the Lord's tender Dealing with him, and helping him fince he vifited him in his young Years, and that the Lord was now with him ; and after remembring his dear Love to Friends, as apprehenfive his End drew near; he faid, *His Way was bright and clear before him, and that he was truly refigned to the Will of the Lord.*

He

He died at *Palmer*'s Green near *Edmond-ton*, in *Middlesex*, the 16th of the Ninth Month 1721, and was buried on the 21st of the same in Friends Burial-ground near *Bunhill-fields*, after a Meeting at the *Bull and Mouth* Meeting-house, attended by a numerous Company of Friends and friendly People. Aged about fifty-five Years.

GEORGE BOWLES, formerly of *Giles Chalfont*, within the Compass of *Jourdan*'s Meeting in *Buckinghamshire*, was convinced of Truth in *London*, about the Year 1681. He was a Man whom the Lord favour'd with a good Understanding, and although he had not much human Learning, yet he was eminently endued with divine Gifts, whereby he was qualified and made an able Minister of the Everlasting Gospel, and under the Influences thereof was enabled to declare the Doctrine of Truth in a living powerful Testimony, to that Divine Light, which leads to Salvation. His Doctrine was sound, instructive, very solid, and free from Affectation, tendering the Hearts of the Hearers. He was not only serviceable in Ministry, but was eminently so in the Discipline and Government of the Church, in which he was frequently con-

C   cern'd

cern'd, and zealous that nothing might remain which would eclipfe the Luftre and
Beauty thereof ; and that all who profeffed
the Truth might walk worthy thereof. Thus
fweetly did he walk through a Courfe of
many Years ; and when through bodily Infirmities
rendered incapable of getting to
Meeting, which was a Mile from his Houfe,
he removed to *High-wickham*, that he might
be near the Meeting-houfe.

About five Days before his Death, he
was feized with a ftrong *Fever*, in which the
Lord was pleafed to be with him to the
Comfort of Friends, who were about him.

The Evening before his End, he was
open'd in Spirit to fpeak in Lamentation
of the unhappy State of many, who through
Unwatchfulnefs, and by lending an Ear to
the Enemy, had neglected thofe great Privileges
God in his Mercy had offered them,
in order for their Everlafting Good ; and alfo
of the Lord's Goodnefs, declaring his Love
in preferving the Faithful in Ages paft, and
even down to this Day : And concluding
with a fweet Supplication to the Lord.

He departed this Life on the 18th of the
Eleventh Month 1721, and his Body accompanied
by Friends, was interred in their
Burial-

Burial-ground at *New-Jourdans*, the 22d of the fame.

CHRISTIAN BARCLAY, of *Ury* in *Scotland*, Widow of *Robert Barclay*, (Author of the Apology) to whom fhe was married in the Year 1669, and fur-vived him thirty-two Years, was Daughter of *Gilbert Molleson*, of *Aberdeen*, Merchant, and *Margaret* his Wife, whofe pious Life is recorded in a former Treatife of this fort : She was born in 1647, and by Accounts preferved was religioufly inclined from her Youth, and publickly embraced the Tefti-mony of Truth about the fixteenth Year of her Age, and through many Hardfhips and Sufferings, walked in a fteady Converfation confiftent with her Profeffion ; her Care and Concern was great, that all who profeffed the Truth might poffefs it ; grave, ferious and weighty in Converfation, diligent in Bufinefs, and fervent in Spirit, being often attended with the Power and Prefence of Divine Goodnefs, in which many precious Opportunities of Refrefhment to many pre-fent were plentifully manifefted and experi-enced, both in her Company and under her Miniftry, to their great Joy and Comfort.

C 2   Her

Her Care and Concern was great to prevent Slackneſs or Indifferency in the Church, but that Diligence might be uſed to make our Calling and Election ſure ; her daily Concern for her Children and Grand-Children, that they might be preſerv'd, was evident to all ; her Care to aſſiſt the Poor and ſupply them with Neceſſaries, eſpecially the Sick, left laſting Impreſſions on their Minds of Love and Regard.

She was taken ill the 12th of the Ninth Month 1722, and from that Time continued in a weak State, in which ſhe witneſſed many comfortable Opportunities ; her Concern for the Truth and Churches Proſperity continued with her to the laſt, for Sickneſs ſeem'd not to alter her Temper or Concern : Many pious Expreſſions dropt from her during her Ilneſs, and he who had been with her all her Life long, bleſſed her with his Preſence to the drawing of her laſt Breath, which appear'd to be in great Peace and Quietneſs, the 14th of the Twelfth Month 1722. Aged ſeventy-ſix Years.

GEORGE

GEORGE WHITEHEAD, of the City of *London*, was one who in the firſt breaking forth of Truth in this Nation, as profeſſed by the People called *Quakers*, was raiſed up in his very young Years to bear Teſtimony thereto, and thro' laborious and exerciſing Travel, became inſtrumental in the firſt planting thereof, about the City of *Norwich* and Parts adjacent; and having been conducted through a long Courſe of Years, unſpotted to his Concluſion, for the Encouragement of all who may read this Account, the following Extract, from the Teſtimony of *Devonſhire - houſe* Monthly Meeting concerning him, of which he was a very ſerviceable Member for about fifty Years, is thought worthy a Place in theſe Memoirs.

" He was born at *Sun-big*, in the Pariſh
" of *Orton*, in the County of *Weſtmoreland*,
" about the Year 1636, of honeſt Parents,
" who gave him Education in Grammar
" Learning.

" At or about the ſeventeenth Year of his
" Age, when Friends, by the mighty Power
" of God, were gathered to be a People,
" the

" the Lord was pleafed to vifit him, and
" by the Teftimony of Truth, he was
" reached unto, and convinced of the Ne-
" ceffity of an inward and fpiritual Work
" to be known and wrought upon the Souls
" of Men; and of the Emptinefs of out-
" ward Shew and Formality in Religion:
" And in the Year 1654, and the eighteenth
" Year of his Age, the Lord fent him forth
" to preach the Everlafting Gofpel in Life
" and Power; and having paffed through
" *York*, *Lincoln* and *Cambridge*, travelling
" on Foot, had fome Service in his Journey.
" He came while a Youth into *Norfolk* and
" *Suffolk*, where he vifited fome few Meet-
" ings of Friends and fober Profeffors; at
" one of which, near the whole Meeting was
" convinced, by the mighty Power of God,
" through his lively and piercing Teftimony
" and Prayer.

" He continued fome Months in *Norfolk*,
" and about *Norwich*, where having Meet-
" ings, he preached the Everlafting Gofpel,
" and thereby turn'd many from Darknefs
" to Light, and from the Power of Sin and
" Satan, unto God and his Power; that
" People might not continue in empty Forms
" and Shadows, but come to the Life and
" Subftance of true Religion; and to know
" Chrift their true Teacher and Leader:
" And

" And great was his Service, Labour and
" Travel in thofe Counties, whereby many
" were reached unto, convinced of, and
" eftablifhed in the bleffed Truth ; and
" fome raifed up to bear a publick Tefti-
" mony thereunto : But he fuffered great
" Oppofition, Hardfhips, long and fore Im-
" prifonments, and fevere Whipping for his
" Teftimony to the Truth, in thofe his ten-
" der Years," as by his Journal of more
than 600 Pages ; wherein many of his
Services and Travels throughout moft Parts
of this Nation are largely related, will
appear.

" He was one whom the Lord had fitly
" qualified and prepared, by his Divine
" Power and Holy Spirit, for that Work
" whereunto he was called ; and whereby
" he was made an able Minifter of the
" Gofpel : He was a large Experiencer of
" the Work of God, and deep Myfteries
" of the Heavenly Kingdom, and was fre-
" quently opened in Meetings to declare of,
" and unfold the fame in the clear Demon-
" ftration of the Spirit and Power, dividing
" the Word aright, to the opening and
" convincing the Underftandings of many,
" who were unacquainted with the Way and
" Work of Truth, and to the comforting,
" confirming and eftablifhing of the People
" and

" and Children of the Lord in their Journey
" and Travel Zion-ward.

" He was not only a zealous Contender
" for, and Afferter of the true Faith and
" Doctrine of our Lord and Saviour Jefus
" Chrift, in a found and intelligible Tefti-
" mony, but alfo was valiant and fkilful
" in the Defence thereof, againft Adverfa-
" ries and Oppofers of the fame ; and one,
" who through a long Courfe of many
" Days, was careful to adorn the Doctrine
" of our Holy Profeffion, by a circumfpect
" Life and godly Converfation, wherein the
" Fruits of the Spirit, _viz._ Love, Joy,
" Peace, Long-fuffering, Gentlenefs, Good-
" nefs, Faith, Meeknefs and Temperance,
" did eminently fhine forth through him,
" to the Praife and Glory of God.

" Being thus qualify'd, and of a meek
" and peaceable Difpofition, he was had
" in good Efteem amongft moft Sorts of
" People that were acquainted with him ;
" which tended much to the opening his
" Way in his publick Service for Truth,
" and frequent Solicitations of the King and
" Parliament, Bifhops and great Men in
" his Time, for the Relief and Releafe of
" his fuffering Friends and Brethren, under
" fore Perfecutions and hard Imprifonments,
" and

" and for Liberty of Conscience, and also
" for Relief in case of Oaths : In which
" Labour of Love and eminent Services,
" among other Brethren, this our dear
" Friend was principally exercised, and the
" Lord was with him, and made way for
" him in the Hearts of the Rulers ; so that
" his faithful Labour was often crown'd
" with Success, to the comforting and re-
" joicing of the Hearts of many suffering
" Brethren.

" He was a good Example to the Flock
" in his diligent frequenting of First and
" Week-day Meetings for publick Worship,
" and other Meetings for the Service of
" Truth, so long as his Ability of Body
" remain'd ; willing to take all Opportu-
" nities for publishing and promoting the
" Truth ; zealous to support good Order,
" and Discipline in the Church of Christ :
" And as he was not suddenly for taking
" hold of any, so he was as exemplary in
" not being forward to cast any off, in
" whom there appeared any thing that was
" good, being always desirous to encourage
" the Good in all, condescending to the
" Weak, but admonishing the Faulty, in
" the Spirit of Meekness and Wisdom,
" that they might be preserved in Love to

D   " Truth,

" Truth, and come into the *Unity of the one*
" *Spirit, which is the Bond of Peace.*

" He was a tender Father in the Church,
" and as such was of great Compassion,
" sympathizing with the Afflicted whether
" in Body or Mind ; a diligent Visiter of
" the Sick, and labouring to comfort the
" mourning Soul ; careful to prevent, and
" diligent in composing Differences.

" It pleased the Lord to visit him with
" some severe Pains and Weakness of Body,
" so that he was disabled for some Weeks
" from getting to Meetings ; but he often
" expressed his Desires for the Welfare of
" the Church of Christ, and that Friends
" might live in Love and Unity.

" He continued in a patient resigned
" Frame of Mind to the Will of God,
" waiting for his great Change, rather de-
" siring to be *dissolved and be with Christ,*
" saying, *the Sting of Death was taken away.*

" He expressed a little before his De-
" parture, *That he had a renewed Sight or*
" *Remembrance of his Labours and Travels,*
" *that he had gone through from his first*
" *Convincement ; he looked upon them with*
" *abundance of Comfort and Satisfaction, and*
" admired

" *admired how the Presence of the Lord had*
" *attended and carried him through them all.*

" He departed this Life in great Peace
" and Quiet the 8th Day of the First
" Month 1722-3, about the eighty-seventh
" Year of his Age, having been a Minister
" about sixty-eight Years, and was buried
" the 13th of the same in Friends Burial-
" ground in *Bunhill-fields*, attended by a
" large Number of his Friends and others."

THOMAS ALDAM, formerly
of *Warmsworth* in *Yorkshire*, was educated in the Way of Truth we profess: He
was in his Youth early visited with the spiritual Appearance thereof in his Soul, and by
and through Faithfulness thereunto he was
fitted and prepared for a Dispensation of the
Gospel about the twenty-fourth Year of his
Age ; in which he was fervent in stirring up
Friends to Faithfulness in the several Testi-
monies of Truth, and which he also adorn'd
with an exemplary Life and Conversation,
giving Testimony thereto by two Years and
an half's Imprisonment, about the Years
1671 and 1684.

D 2   He.

He was diligent in attending Meetings both for Worship and Discipline, in which he was very serviceable, being of a sound Judgment and able in Counsel. Much might be said of his Labours, in which he always sought the Preservation of Peace, and Unity among Friends, and retain'd his Integrity to old Age.

He was taken ill about the Seventh Month 1722, and from that Time kept his Room under great Weakness of Body; but was preserved in a weighty tender Frame of Spirit. And as he had always been a diligent Attender of Meetings, so at his Desire the Meeting was often kept in his Room; in which he was fervent in Prayer, and bore Testimony to the Goodness of God to his Soul; and had a Word of Encouragement and Exhortation to others, to their mutual Comfort and Edification. During his Ilness he was frequently visited by Friends, to some of whom he expressed his *Hope and Confidence in the Lord, that through the Mercy of God in Christ Jesus, he should have a Place of Rest in the World to come, and an Inheritance among those who are sanctified.*

He departed this Life the 17th of the First Month 1722-3, and was buried in the Burying-place at *Warmsworth,* which himself had

had inclofed and built a Meeting-houfe therein, and in his Life-time given to the Ufe of Friends, the 19th of the fame. Aged feventy-four Years.

RICHARD CLARIDGE, was born in the Tenth Month 1649, at *Farmborough* in the County of *Warwick*, of fober and reputable Parents, who brought him up to Learning from his Childhood, and in the feventeenth Year of his Age fent him to the Univerfity of *Oxford*; where after fome Years Continuance, he took his Degree of *B. A.* and was ordain'd a Deacon. In the Year 1672, he was ordain'd a Prieft, and had his Induction to the Rectory of *Peopleton* in the faid County of *Warwick*, where he continued a publick Preacher upwards of nineteen Years.

During which Time, the Lord was often pleafed by the Infhining of his Divine Light, to open his Underftanding, and fhewed him the Inconfiftency of his then Employment; and for the Sake of a good Confcience towards God, he quitted his parochial Charge and Tithe Revenue, and freely refign'd the Service in the Year 1691.

After

After which he join'd himself to the *Baptists*, and was for some Time a publick Preacher among them; but his seeking Soul not finding that Satisfaction which he earnestly longed for and sought after, his Eye being still to the Lord for the Guidance and Direction of his Holy Spirit, the Mystery of the pure evangelical Dispensation was clearly manifested, and he was brought to embrace the Truth as professed by us, and made a publick Profession thereof in the Year 1697, and was brought to a patient Waiting in Silence, not daring again to open his Mouth until it pleased the Lord by the immediate Operation of his blessed Spirit to influence him thereto, and make him a free Minister of the Gospel of Christ; in which his Testimony was found and edifying, pressing all to Purity of Life, adorning the same in his Life and Conversation; in which his Piety towards God and Love to his Neighbour, the Truth and Justice of his Words and Actions, made him as a Light in the World, and gave forth a Testimony to the Truth in the Hearts of others. In his own Family he was a living Example of Virtue, being an affectionate Husband, a loving Father, and a kind and gentle Master; frequent in Supplication to the Lord for the Preservation of himself and Houshold in the Way of Truth and Righteousness, charitable

to

to the Poor, and a frequent Visiter of the Sick ; and in his more publick Service, his various Treatises wrote in Defence of Truth, will stand as lasting Monuments of his unwearied Endeavours for its Promotion.

For some Years before his Death, he was in a declining State as to bodily Health, yet his Love and Zeal declined not ; but he kept close to Meetings till about a Week before his Departure, when he was taken with a Shortness of Breath attended with a *Fever,* which continued on him to his End. During the Time of his Sickness he expressed to divers Friends who visited him, his *inward Peace and Satisfaction of Soul, and an humble Resignation to the Divine Will, in an assured Hope of a glorious Immortality, placing his whole Trust and Confidence in the free Grace and Mercy of God.*

He departed this Life the 28th of the Second Month 1723, aged seventy-three Years, and was buried in Friends Burial-ground near *Bunhill-fields,* accompanied by a numerous Company of Friends and others.

JOHN

JOHN BROWN, an ancient Friend in the County of *Surry*, was born at *Laleham* in *Midddlesex*, the 1st of the Sixth Month 1639, and was one of the first convinced in the County where he dwelt, and became a Member of the Monthly-meeting of *Kingston upon Thames* when the Meeting-house was built, and continued a Member thereof forty-eight Years; being according to the Talent received, a zealous Contender for the Faith, not fearing the Face of Man, nor turning his Back in the Day of Battle; but patiently suffered Imprisonment in *Newgate* six or seven Times, as well as other Goals, one of which was before the Fire of *London*, when he was obliged to carry his Bed out on his Back, when the Prison was burnt; besides the Spoiling of Goods which he many Times suffer'd: And he neither fled in the Winter, nor on the Sabbath-day; but remained steadfast to the Truth to the Day of his Death.

He was taken ill at his Son-in-Law's *Jacob Forsters*'s, in *Blackman-street, Southwark,* about the Fourth Month 1723, which he endured with great Patience and Satisfaction, being sensible it was for his End, and expressed

preſſed his Reſignation thereto, full of Heavenly Expreſſions and Divine Exhortations to all who were about him.

He died the 6th of the Fifth Month 1723, and was buried in Friends Burial-ground at *Kingſton* aforeſaid. Aged upwards of eighty-two Years.

DANIEL ROBERTS, an ancient Friend, of *Cheſham* in the County of *Bucks*, was born at *Siddington* near *Cirenceſter*, in the County of *Glouceſter*, about the Year 1656 ; his Father *John Roberts*, of the ſame Place, was convinced in the firſt breaking forth of Truth as profeſſed by us, by that Servant of Chriſt *Richard Farnſworth*, of whom ſome Memoirs are extant. This our worthy Friend was one whom in his early Age the Lord was pleaſed to call into his Vineyard, and committed a Diſpenſation of the Goſpel to him ; in the Exerciſe of which he was often made an Inſtrument of Edification and Comfort, and by his Labour therein ſome were convinced before his Removal to *Cheſham* ; and he not only had to do, but to ſuffer for his Teſtimony, being impriſoned in *Glouceſter* Caſtle about two Years, till diſcharged about the Year 1684.

E

After

After his Settlement at *Chesham*, great was his Care to shew forth an exemplary Conversation of a meek and peaceable Spirit, seeking the Peace and Unity of the Church, being often opened in tender Counsel to the Weak, yet steady in his Zeal against every Appearance of Evil. In his Family a loving Husband, a tender Father, and a kind Master : To his Neighbours courteous and kind, his honest and innocent Conversation raising an honourable Esteem for him.

In his last Ilness he appeared to be in a sweet Frame of Mind, much to the Comfort of some Friends who visited him, and gave them good Cause to believe he died in Peace with the Lord and enter'd into Rest.

He departed this Life the 16th of the Twelfth Month 1726, and was interred in Friends Burial-ground the 19th of the same. Aged about 70 Years.

J A M E S.

JAMES OLDHAM, was born at *Warrington* in the County of *Lancaster*, about the Year 1715, his Conversation was *according to the Course of this World, and according to the Prince of the Power of the Air, the Spirit that now worketh in the Children of Disobedience,* until about the twentieth Year of his Age, when reading some Books on religious Subjects, he perceived the Necessity of experiencing Judgment because of Sin, and the Work of Redemption through Jesus Christ our Lord. After having been for some Time seeking the Way to Zion, according to the Degrees of Light and Knowledge imparted, he was convinced of the Truth professed by the People called *Quakers,* and became a deeply exercised, exemplary and well-approved Member of their Society.

The Awfulness and Simplicity of his Conduct is still remembred by some, to whom in their religious Infancy he was as a nursing Father, although himself but a Stripling in respect to Years. Having tasted that the Lord was gracious, he had strong Sympathy with the sincere Travailers under various Denominations; nevertheless he was

very

very careful not to go before or beyond the Guidance of Truth for the Help of others.

Being seized with a *Fever*, at some Intervals his Understanding was affected; but at others the Composure and Solemnity of his Spirit was comfortably apparent: He addressed divers of his Friends in a manner suitable to their States, and signified his sole Dependance was upon that merciful Arm whereby he had been visited. The Day before his Decease, a Friend sitting by his Bedside, he bore a short but powerful Testimony to the Love and Goodness of God; expressed the Views he then had of the Divine Light and Glory, adding by way of Appeal to the Almighty, *Oh Lord! thou knowest I have loved thee with an unfeigned Love*; or in Words of like Import.

After some Time spent in solemn Silence, he brake forth into an audible Melody, which was very affecting; and having been singularly cautious of expressing more than he enjoy'd, there is abundant Reason to think he was at that Season favoured with a Sense his Warfare was nearly accomplished, and of a Settlement in the Divine Presence and Favour for ever.

He

He departed this Life at the Houſe of *William Wagſtaffe*, in *Martin's-le-Grand*, in remarkable Quietneſs as a Lamb, in the Third Month 1740, aged about twenty-five Years ; and after a large and ſolemn Meeting, was decently interred in Friends Burial-ground in *Bunhill-fields*.

JOHN FOTHERGILL, of *Carrend* in *Wenſleydale*, but late of *Knareſborcugh* in *Yorkſhire*, was born of religious Parents, and carefully educated in the Principles of Truth ; being made ſenſible in his early Years, that neither Tradition, outward Regularity, nor any thing ſhort of real inward Purification of Soul, would render him acceptable in the Sight of the Lord ; he therefore gave up his Heart to him, who through the effectual Operation of his Divine Grace, baptized and gradually purified his Spirit; and prepared and fitted him to be an able Miniſter of the Goſpel of Peace and Salvation ; to which Service he was called when but young, and readily gave up, not ſuffering the Things of this World to take up his Mind and Time ; but labour'd diligently and faithfully therein, from his young Years to the Concluſion of his Days.

In

In all the Stations of Life, his Testimony was confirm'd and adorned by a Conduct becoming a Minister of Christ, whom he served faithfully and with great Diligence; and by a daily inward Dwelling with the Spring of Wisdom and Light, his Mind was often opened, and his Spirit sustain'd to secret Worship when his Hand was upon his Labour. His Delight was in the Law of his God, to meditate therein Day and Night, and to talk of his Statutes in his House to his Family, and those with whom he conversed; and many Times by a Transition from Earthly to Heavenly Things, instructed and edify'd the Minds of those present.

In his publick Testimony, awful and weighty, being endued with true Wisdom, strong and immovably bent against all Unrighteousness; quick in discerning, and powerful in detecting the Mysteries of Antichrist, who has sought to stupify the People with the Golden Cup, and thereby to spread the Power, and enlarge the Borders of the Kingdom of Death. As a Flame of Fire was he to the Rebellious and Stubborn; but refreshing as the Dew on *Hermon* to the honest Travailer, ministring Counsel and Comfort to the drooping Soul; being not only an Instructor, but a Father to many; zealous and wise in the Support of the Discipline

pline eftablifhed amongft us ; impartially
and honeftly doing Judgment and Juftice:
No Family Connections (not even his own)
could bias him from laying the Line upon
Offenders, nor from a fteady Endeavour to
keep clean the Camp of God ; in which
Labour, he was often fuccefsful, being made
a Terror to evil Doers, and a Praife to them
that did well.

Thus conducted in every Station of Life,
he became honourable amongft Men, and
greatly efteem'd by thofe of fuperior Rank
who knew him ; being adorn'd with that
Dignity which Truth confers on its faithful
Followers.

In the Courfe of his Gofpel Labours he
travelled much in this Nation, in *Scotland*
and *Wales:* He vifited *Ireland* feveral Times,
and thrice he, croffed the. Seas to *America*
in the fame Service, to the Comfort and
Edification of the Churches, leaving Seals of
his Miniftry in many Places. In the Year
1744 he attended the Yearly-meeting at
London, in Company with his ancient Friend
Bofwell Middleton, for whom he had a fingular Efteem ; and altho' his Weaknefs
rendred it difficult for him to attend the
large Meetings for Bufinefs, neverthelefs he.
did attend them, and his exemplary, reve-
rent,

rent, watchful Frame of Mind therein, rendred his Company truly acceptable and serviceable. On his Return he attended the Midfummer Quarterly - meeting at *York* ; after which in a Letter to a Friend, after mentioning the Weakneſs of his Body, " Yet," ſays he, " I think my better Part " is almoſt uncommonly ſupply'd in divers " Reſpects, much to my Comfort, and the " reviving of my Faith in the Heavenly In- " fluence, which is Strength in Weakneſs, " and will be, where his only worthy Name " hath the Praiſe."

In the latter Part of the ſaid Year he at- tended the circular Yearly-meeting at *Wor- ceſter*, where he was enabled to bear a noble *Chriſtian* Teſtimony to the All-ſufficiency of that Power which had preſerved, ſupported and guided him in the Way that was right and well-pleaſing ; and is likewiſe able to do the ſame for all the Children of Men. And after viſiting *Briſtol*, *Bath*, and ſome other Meetings, he return'd Home by eaſy Jour- neys, having Meetings as Opportunities offer'd ; after his Return he got to Meetings for ſome Weeks, and his Teſtimony was as lively and powerful as ever ; ſeveral Times expreſſing his Satisfaction and inward Peace, in having perform'd his laſt Journey, ſaying, *His Shoulders were a good deal lighten'd by it,*

and

and he was reconciled to his Grave if he was now to be taken away.

The two laſt Weeks he ſlept almoſt continually, Day and Night, his Memory and Capacity being much impair'd ; yet when almoſt all other Expreſſions fail'd, he was obſerv'd to repeat the following, in a very fervent and emphatical manner : *Heavenly Goodneſs is near, Heavenly Goodneſs is near.* Thus, the mighty God who viſited him in his Youth with the Diſcovery of his ſaving Power, who thereby cleanſed him from Unrighteouſneſs, and ſanctify'd him to himſelf as a choſen Veſſel, ſupported him in all his faithful Labours by Sea and Land, covered his Head in all Conflicts, and by whom his Bow abode in Strength, became his Evening Song and Stay in the Decline of Life ; that Heavenly Goodneſs he had ever prized as his chiefeſt Joy, remained as a Seal upon his Spirit, that he had pleaſed God, and was accepted of him.*

He departed this Life at *Knareſborough*, the 13th of the Eleventh Month 1744, and was honourably buried in Friends Burying-

* For a further Account of this worthy Man, ſee a new Edition of his Journal.

F   ground

ground at *Scotten* near the said Town, the 15th of the said Month. Aged sixty-nine, a Minister near fifty Years.

BENJAMIN KIDD, of *Banbury* in *Oxfordshire*, was born at or near *Settle* in the County of *York*, and was educated among Friends; and while very young was favour'd with a Visitation of Truth, to which he was faithful, and thro' the powerful Operation thereof, was in or about the twenty-first Year of his Age called to the Work of the Ministry; wherein he was eminently qualified rightly to divide the Word of Truth, and to unfold the Mysteries of the Gospel in great Brightness, to the Informing and Convincing many, and to the Comfort and Encouragement of such as were under Affliction and Distress of Mind in their religious Progress.

He was eminently qualified for great and singular Services in the Church, a diligent Attender of Meetings, both for Worship and Discipline; in both which he was very serviceable. A Man of great Sincerity and Integrity, of good Understanding in Matters useful to Mankind, and freely communicative; universal in his Benevolence,

and

and laborious to do Good to all. Deep in Divine Experience, found in Judgment, wife in Counfel, zealous for the Promotion of Truth and Righteoufnefs, and the Exaltation of the Caufe of his Lord and Mafter in the Earth ; inftructive and weighty, yet becomingly chearful in Converfation ; exemplary in Life and Conduct, peculiarly kind and fatherly towards his Friends, compaffionate to the Poor and Diftreffed, generous and noble in his Difpofition, highly ufeful and agreeable to his Neighbours, and generally beloved by Perfons of all Ranks and Denominations to whom he was known.

The principal Defign of thefe Obfervations is to excite thee, Reader, to confider in what manner he was raifed to this Dignity in the Church ; and alfo to reflect, that the fame Divine Principle is in thee, and if thou art faithful thereto, the fame Fruits will appear according to thy Meafure.

About the thirtieth Year of his Age, he vifited *America*, where many were convinced, and others confirmed through his powerful Miniftry. His Service there was very great, and much to the Edification, Comfort, and Satisfaction of Friends, as appears from fundry Accounts.

After

After he settled at *Banbury*, he visited *Ireland* and various Parts of this Nation: The City of *London* in particular, frequently partook of his pious and fervent Labours, to the great Help and Consolation of many, who have had just Reason to bless the Lord on his Behalf.

A few Months before his Death he was greatly afflicted with the *Stone*, which was very painful to bear; but at Times he got a little out, and particulary he attended the Quarterly-meeting at *Oxford* in the Tenth Month 1750, O. S. though under great Affliction of Body, which gradually increased, together with a *Dropsical* Disorder attending; through all which, his Patience and Resignation were very remarkable. About a Month before his Decease, he attended the Meeting at *Banbury*, at the Burial of a young Man whom he greatly esteemed, which he got to with great Difficulty, being obliged to be supported by two Friends. In the Course of the Meeting, he was raised beyond all Expectation to preach the Gospel powerfully for about an Hour, to the tendring the Hearts of almost all present; many of his Neighbours being there, confessed with Admiration, to the Power by which he was raised that Day, remarking, *That he had been a good Man all his Time, and that the*
Almighty

Almighty had crown'd him in the Conclusion. After this he was mostly confined within Doors, and continued in great Submission to the Divine Will, without murmuring or repining.

A Friend from *London* visiting him, found him under great bodily Affliction, but freely resign'd to the Divine Will ; expressing *His firm Hope in that Power which had all along supported him, and that though the greatest Kindness to him, was to solicit a Release from his Pains, yet he desired to be content and wait the Lord's Time* ; and when the said Friend took his Leave of him, he expressed himself to him in an affectionate manner to his great Comfort and Encouragement.

At another Time, having deliver'd some excellent Exhortations to those present with him, he added for their Encouragement to persevere in their *Christian* Progress, *I am under no Fear nor doubtful Apprehensions ; for I know, that for me to live is Christ, and to die is Gain.*

When he was first seized with the *Hiccough*, he seem'd full of Joy, saying, *This is a welcome Messenger, it is one Step nearer :* His Wife standing by, asking Why ? He answered, *It will be a glorious Change, I am*

not

*not afraid to die and to put on Immortality;
that will be desirable, yet I leave it, though
of Choice I had rather be dissolved ; but the
Lord's Time will be the best Time : Often
saying, Death would be the most welcome
Messenger he ever met with.*

Thus this good Man finished his Course,
his Sun going down in great Brightness, at
Ranbury, the 21st of the Third Month 1751,
O. S. and was buried the 24th of the same,
after a large and solemn Meeting. Aged
about fifty-nine, a Minister about thirty-
eight Years.

S ARAH ARTIS, was born at
Woodbridge in the County of *Suffolk*, in
the Year 1714, of religious Parents, who
were both taken away while she was young.
She early discover'd a sincere Desire after the
Knowledge of the Truth, and the Seed
thereof falling upon good Ground it took
Root downward ; and being humble in
Spirit, and patient under the Operations of
it, it brought forth plentifully ; so that about
the twenty-sixth Year of her Age she came
forth in Testimony, in which she was clear
in her Delivery, sound in Judgment, and
being seasoned with Gospel Love, it might
truly

truly be faid, fhe was one of the wife-hearted Women in our *Ifrael.*

She was often concern'd to vifit Particulars, more especially of the younger Sort; and was often made inftrumental to the Opening their prefent States, and to adminifter the Wine and the Oil as the Occafion required. She vifited divers Parts of this Nation and *Ireland,* and her Life and Converfation corresponding with the Doctrine fhe preach'd, her Services therein were acceptable.

Her Ilnefs, which was a *Cancer* in her Mouth, was very long, and much affected her Speech, that fhe could not utter Words but with great Difficulty; and as fhe languifhed for fome Months, and was earneft in Spirit that fhe might be preferved in the Patience to an entire Refignation, whether to live or die.

She expreffed great Satisfaction in that fhe had been faithful in the Difcharge of her Duty; and near her Latter-end had a great Defire of being diffolved, in a full Affurance of entering into that Reft which is prepared for them that die in the Lord.

She departed this Life about the forty-fourth Year of her Age, and was interred in Friends

Friends Burial-ground at *Woodbridge*, the 19th of the Fourth Month 1758. A Minister eighteen Years.

WILLIAM PITTS, of *Southwark*, in his young Years was early visited with a Call of Divine Grace, and by adhering thereto and submitting to its Operations, he became convinced of the essential Doctrines of *Christianity* as professed by us; and though in his Minority he was educated by a Priest, under whose Tuition he attain'd a considerable Knowledge in several of the learned Languages; yet the tender Scruples which were raised in his Mind, under a clear Conviction of the Impropriety of the needless Ceremonies and Salutations in which he had been educated, exposed him to many Sufferings from his Father, from whom he received unkind Treatment, which he endured with much Patience and Fortitude; and which tended much to his Growth and Advancement in religious Experience, and Preparation for further Service.

From some Minutes he left, he was under some Conflict of Mind respecting his appearing in the Ministry, which continued near three Years before he gave up thereto; and

having

having a clear Senfe of the Importance of that weighty Service, and the Neceffity of obtaining a certain Evidence of his Miffion, he waited for a Confirmation thereof, left he fhould run before he was fent. In the Fifth Month 1738 he was enabled to utter the following Sentence, *If the Trumpet give an uncertain Sound, who can prepare himfelf for the Battle* ; which, as he has been heard to fay, *afforded him Inftruction through the future Service of his Day*, which was very great, his Heart being fully given up to do whatever his Hand might find to do, as was evident from his own Expreffions to fome Friends who vifited him in his Ilnefs, whom he encouraged to Faithfulnefs, faying, *That for the laft twenty Years he had never omitted one Service which had appeared to be his Duty, and he had now the Comfort and Satisfaction thereof :* Or Words to that Effect ; and great were his Services, his Talents and Qualifications were employ'd to the Glory of the Giver.

In the Fourth Month 1760 he fet out to vifit Friends in *Buckinghamfhire*, and fome adjacent Parts ; but being much indifpofed he returned homewards, and at the Houfe of our Friend *Thomas Goring*, at *Uxbridge*, he was fuddenly taken very ill ; during which he uttered the following Expreffions, *Oh my*

G   *Father !*

Father ! my Father ! be pleased to be with me in my Affliction : And he gave it as his Judgment, that *his Time in this World would be short, and that he should die of this present Illness ;* and said, *I am fully resigned to the Will of Providence ;* declaring, *he coveted not Length of Days,* and that *he was very easy in Body and Mind.* Being asked how he did, he said, *he was very weak in Body, but I have a great Physician in Heaven, who is very merciful to me, and near me in this Illness.* At another Time, after having repeated his perfect Resignation to the Will of his great Master, said, *But if it pleased him, he had rather die than live, unless he had any further Service for him to do :* And he could rejoice, saying, *O Death, where is thy Sting ? O Grave, where is thy Victory ? The Sting of Death is Sin, and the Strength of Sin is the Law ; but Thanks be to God, who giveth as the Victory.* Many Friends from *London* and elsewhere went to see him, whose Visits he took very kind, and to one of them he expressed himself in the following manner : *I never coveted Riches nor Power ; and indeed if I had obtained them, what could they, or all the Friendships of the World do for me now ? Nothing but the Testimony of a pure Conscience, and the inward Sense of Divine Favour, can comfort my Soul in these Moments ; and Thanks be to my Heavenly Father,*

Father, I feel his supporting Arm underneath, and it is a Rest indeed, a Joy that overcomes all ; it makes this Bed easy, and enables me to bear calmly, and without Complaint, the Dispensations of his gracious Providence ; I wish for nothing to myself otherwise than it is. I accept with Satisfaction and Thanks the Kindness of my Friends : In Compliance with their Request, and thinking it my Duty to do what may be in my Power, I take the Medicines prescribed, which though it may not seem meet to Providence in his Wisdom, to render instrumental in the Restoration of Health ; yet through his Blessing they have so far succeeded, as to remove the Sense of acute Pain. To be thoughtful of, and prepare for this trying Time, have I frequently and earnestly exhorted others ; not without considering and knowing the many and strong Temptations of this World ; which however, as we are obedient to the Spirit of Christ, we shall be enabled to overcome ; that in the Conclusion they might have this Answer of Peace, this Divine Consolation of Mind : And it always appeared best to me, to do this in great Love and Gentleness, so that I might perswade, not force them to Christ. When this Time comes, it will be found hard Work, without any Additional Weight, to struggle on a Dying-bed with the Pangs of the Body. But how much more to be lamented is the Condition of those, whose

G 2 *Consciences*

Confciences accufe them with having enriched themfelves by oppreffing the Poor and Helplefs; and when in an unprepared State, after a Life of Rebellion and hardened in Iniquity, fuch muft feel the Terrors of a guilty Mind, added to the Agonies of a perifhing Body.

A Friend who went to vifit him, a Day before his Death, afked him how he did; after a fhort Paufe he faid, *I am waiting for my great Change : O my Father ! be pleafed to be with me, and comfort me in my laft Moments.* The laft Words he was heard to fpeak were thefe : *There is a great God in Heaven, who is Zion's King : O Zion ! O Zion ! O thou great King of Kings !* Soon after which he departed in great Tranquility and Compofure of Mind, the 15th of the Fifth Month 1760. His Body was brought to his own Houfe in *Blacks-fields, Southwark*; and from thence, after a folemn Meeting at *Horflydown*, attended by many Friends, decently interred at Friends Burial-ground in the *Park, Southwark*. Aged about fifty-one Years, and a Minifter twenty-two Years.

ROBERT

ROBERT PLUMSTED, of *Grace-church-ftreet, London*, was in his Youth addicted to Gaiety and the delufive Pleafures of this tranfitory World ; but was preferved out of the grofs Evils thereof. About the twenty-eighth Year of his Age, it pleafed Divine Providence in great Mercy to manifeft to him, that if he would obtain Peace he muft walk in the narrow Path of Self-denial : Thus by adhering to the Dictates of Divine Grace, he was enabled to deny himfelf of the Pleafures and Pomps of this World, take up his Crofs, and in a good degree was brought into Conformity to the Leadings of Truth. Sometimes for about a Year before his Deceafe, he appeared in a few Words in our religious Affemblies in a tender manner, which was acceptable to Friends.

He was afflicted with a long and painful Ilnefs, in which he had at Times Accefs to the Throne of Grace, and when reduced very low, uttered thefe Words diftinctly : *Lord ! as thou haft continued me to this Moment, let me not depart without undoubted Evidence of thy Favour.*

He

He quietly departed this Life the 14th of the Seventh Month 1760, at the Hot-Wells near *Briftol*, and his Corps being brought to *London*, was interr'd the 23d of the fame, at *Winchmore-hill*, in *Middlefex*, accompany'd by many Friends, after a large and folemn Meeting at *Devonfhire-houfe* in *London*. Aged thirty-fix Years.

LYDIA LANCASTER, was the Daughter of *Thomas* and *Dorothy Rawlinfon*, of *Graithwaite* in the County of *Lancafter*, who both defcended from Families reputable among Men; and they both came among Friends on the Principle of Convincement, and were religioufly concern'd to inftruct and example their Children therein, as the moft precious of all Bleffings.

That powerful Hand which can alone give the Increafe, mercifully extended an excellent Bleffing to feveral of their Children, and particularly to this their Daughter; and as it opened the Heart of *Lydia* of old, fo it opened hers, to receive the Heavenly Meffage. In her young Years fhe became fenfibly acquainted with the Lord, and witneffed his gracious Dealings with her, in order to redeem

redeem her to himself, and make her a sanctified Vessel to place his Name in.

About the fourteenth Year of her Age, she had a View of the Will of Providence to engage her in the ministerial Service; under which Concern she continued about ten Years, growing in Wisdom and Experience that she might come forth in the right Time, endued with proper Qualifications: In this Time of deep Travail and Heavenly Discipline, she learn'd to say with the Prophet *Isaiah*, Chap. l. Verf. 4. *He wakeneth me Morning by Morning, he wakeneth mine Ear to hear as the Learned.*

About the twenty-fourth Year of her Age, she came forth in a living powerful Testimony, and grew therein; the blessed Author of all spiritual Riches having abundantly replenish'd her with the Treasures of his Kingdom, she soon became an able Dispenser thereof to the Churches, having a Word in due Season to divers States; and like the well-instructed Scribe, brought out of the Treasures committed to her, *Things new and old.* And as she was eminently favour'd by her great Lord and Master, she became humbly devoted to his Requirings; when called forth into the various Parts of his Vineyard,

Vineyard, she freely gave up to spend and be spent for his Cause and Name's Sake.

She visited this Nation or the greatest Part of it several Times, *Ireland* and *Scotland* twice, also the Continent of *America* ; in all which she was render'd instrumental to build up many in the most Holy Faith ; particularly in *America* she left many Seals of her Ministry, both in the Edification and Help of those who were of the Society, and the Convincement of others, gathering them to the great Shepherd of the Flock.

Her Openings into the Mysteries of the Kingdom were deep and instructive, adapted to the State of those amongst whom she labour'd ; close and with Authority to the Negligent and Careless ; yet all her Ministry was attended with that Love and Tenderness which accompany'd her Lord and Master, who *came to seek and to save that which was lost.* She was favour'd with a most excellent Utterance, her Gesture awful, her Voice solemn ; and all her Demeanour in the Exercise of her Gift, becoming the Dignity of the Gospel-Ministry. She was signally favour'd in Supplication, having near Access in Spirit to the Throne of Majesty and Grace, before whom she worshipp'd with calm Rejoicing and awful Reverence.

Thus

Thus through a Courſe of many Years, ſhe retain'd her Zeal and Integrity, and in her old Age ſtrong in the Power of an endleſs Life ; great indeed was her Growth in religious Experience, even to the Stability of Salvation, and an Aſſurance that ſhe ſhould never fall, yet accompanied with the deepeſt Humility. Filial Love which caſts out Fear was the Covering of her Spirit, and reſted almoſt conſtantly upon her for ſeveral Months before her Removal.

About ſix Weeks before her Departure, ſhe thus expreſſed herſelf to a Friend ſhe had favour'd with an intimate Acquaintance : *My natural Strength is not ſo much impair'd as to give me Reaſon to expeƈt a ſudden Removal from this World ; but I feel ſo conſtantly Day and Night the virtuous Life, and my Father's Holy Preſence is ſo conſtantly with me, and I enjoy ſo much the ſpiritual Communion and Fellowſhip of Saints, as to give me an Apprehenſion I am not far from mine Everlaſting Home :* To which ſhe ſweetly added, *A glorious Crown and Everlaſting Song is before me.* (The Friend to whom ſhe thus expreſſed herſelf being deeply affeƈted with the Senſe of the over-ſhadowing of the Holy Wing at that Inſtant of Time) She further added, *If the Foretaſte be ſo joyous, what are the Riches of the Saints Inheritance beyond the Grave !*

H   She

She was supported to labour in the Gospel almost to the Conclusion of her Days, having attended the Funeral of an ancient Friend, *William Backhouse*, several Miles off on the First-day of the Week, and preached the Gospel in the Demonstration of its own Power; and finished her Course the Seventh-day following, and as she lived so she died, in great Favour with God and Man, full of Days and full of Peace.

She died at *Lancaster*, the 30th of the Fifth Month, and was honourably interred in Friends Burial-ground, the 1st of the Sixth Month 1761. Aged about seventy-seven Years, and a Minister about fifty-three Years.

WILLIAM BACKHOUSE, was born in the Year 1695, at *Yea-land* near *Lancaster*, of religious Parents, his Father dying when he was about two Years old, a Prisoner in *Lancaster* Castle, for his conscientious Testimony against the Payment of Tithes, the Education of his Children devolved solely on his Mother, who was religiously concern'd in this Duty, both by Precept and Example, and it pleased Divine Providence

Providence to blefs her Endeavours with Succefs therein.

About the twenty-fixth Year of his Age he came forth in a publick Teftimony, and by faithful Obedience to the Requirings of the Heavenly Giver, he witneffed an Enlargement in his Gift, and was an acceptable Minifter.

He vifited the Churches in moft Parts of this Kingdom, *Scotland*, *Ireland*, and the Continent of *America*, much to the Comfort and Satisfaction of Friends, he being furnifh'd with fufficient Strength for the Service of the Day; being found in Doctrine, tending to Information, Inftruction and Edification; exemplary in attending Meetings both for Worfhip and Difcipline, in the latter of which he was highly ferviceable, being a Lover of Peace, of a loving courteous Difpofition to all, an affectionate Hufband, a tender Parent, and kind Neighbour, which procured the Love and Efteem of them all.

In his laft Ilnefs, being a gradual Decay of Nature, it pleafed the Almighty to favour him with many precious Earnefts of a bleffed Inheritance, divers Friends who vifited him, were in a good degree made fenfible thereof; in fome of thefe Opportunities he

was

was engaged in a lively manner, though in deep Humility, to commemorate the gracious Dealings of the Lord with him in the Course of his Pilgrimage, and thankfully to rejoice that he had labour'd in his Day to perform what he believed required of him ; and could make his Appeal to his Heavenly Master, saying, *Altho' I have had the World to struggle with for the Support and prudent Provision for my Family, yet thou knoweft O Lord ! I have been more concern'd for thy Honour and the good of Souls, than for any other Confiderations.*

Though greatly bleffed in his neareft Connections of Life, yet being wean'd from this World and its Enjoyments, he waited with great Patience and Refignation for his Diffolution.

He departed this Life the 21ft of the Fifth Month 1761, and was buried at *Yealand* the 24th of the fame. Aged fixty-fix, a Minifter above forty Years.

HANNAH

HANNAH SMITH, Wife of *John Smith*, of *Philadelphia*, was the Daughter of *James* and *Sarah Logan*, and born there on the 21ſt of the Twelfth Month 1719-20.

By the Care of her Parents ſhe was in a great Meaſure preſerved from the Levities incident to early Youth, and by the Opportunities of Improvement afterwards, ſhe acquired ſuch Qualifications as gain'd her much Reſpect and Eſteem ; and tho' the affluent Situation in which her Parents were placed, yielded flattering Proſpects of the Eaſe and Gaiety of the World, the durable Riches of true Religion appear'd to her a Treaſure of much more Conſequence, and not to be relinquiſhed for Shadows and Delights that die in the Enjoyment: Thus at a Period when the ſlippery Paths of Vanity in a Succeſſion of increaſing Allurements are apt to enſnare youthful Minds, it pleaſed the Lord to bleſs her Endeavours againſt the Temptations of vain and unprofitable Company, and to ſtrengthen her Love to inward Retirement ; and having taſted of the Viſitation of Divine Love to her Soul, ſhe ſaw it to be the Pearl of great Price, and that her All muſt go to
purchaſe

purchase the Field where it lay ; and from
that Time forward there is Reason to believe
this Purchase became the principal Business of
her Life, and with great Sincerity and Ardour
she labour'd to have all those disquieting
Affections silenced which arise from temporal
Objects, and she was helped at Times to
know the Breathing of her Soul answer'd,
and was made to partake of the Joys of
God's Salvation ; under which her Care over
her Words and Deportment was increased,
and continued to take suitable Opportunities
of Retirement and for reading the Holy
Scriptures ; and in the Relation of a Child,
Wife and Mother, was tenderly careful to
fill up her Place becoming those Stations.

About the Year 1756 she appeared in a
few Words in much Simplicity of Heart
and godly Sincerity, and was concern'd in
visiting Friends in their Families, and also
accompanied some of her own Sex to divers
large Yearly-meetings in the neighbouring
Provinces ; and after her Return to *Philadelphia* (which was half a Year before her
Departure) she continued to attend religious
Meetings, with as much Diligence as the
Weakness of her Constitution would admit,
and when there to clear herself of what she
believed required of her.

During

During the Time of her laſt Ilneſs ſhe told her Huſband ſeveral Times, *That ſhe believed ſhe ſhould not recover;* and though her bodily Pain at Times was very ſharp, ſhe was favour'd with an intire Confidence in the Mercy of God through Jeſus Chriſt, who ſhe found to be a Refuge from Storms, and a ſure Defence in the Day of Diſtreſs. Another Time, acquainting him with great Sweetneſs of Spirit of the State of her Mind, ſhe ſaid, *Notwithſtanding the cloſe Trials I undergo, my Foundation remains ſure, and I have a Hope, yea, an unſhaken Hope, that there is a Place of Reſt prepared for me.* At another Time, ſhe mentioning that the Proſpect of her Change being near, intreated her Huſband to ſtrive for Reſignation, *For,* ſays ſhe, *I am eaſy, I feel no Guilt.* A few Evenings before her Deceaſe, as her Huſband ſat by her Bed-ſide, ſhe deſired that her Children and all about her, might keep as ſtill and quiet as poſſible when ſhe departed, and after mentioning ſeveral other Things relative thereto, told her Huſband, *That ſhe felt Pardon and Forgiveneſs for all Omiſſions of Duty;* and concluded this very affecting Converſation with theſe Words, *Oh the infinite Loving-kindneſs of a merciful God! who has made ſuch a poor Creature as I am, ſo rich in Faith and firm in Hope, that I ſhall be accepted of him.*

She

She departed this Life on the 19th, and was decently interred on the 23d of the Twelfth Month 1761. Aged about forty-one Years.

MARY SLATER, late Wife of *William Slater*, of *Lotherſdale* in *Yorkſhire*, was deſcended of honeſt Parents, though her Mother did not profeſs with us, her Father being after his Marriage convinced of our Principles.

She being of a very gay ſprightly Temper, was ſoon carried away with the deluſive Vanities and Pleaſures which abound, though often attended when very young with ſtrong Convictions; but theſe were ſtifled (for a Time) by various Scenes of Diſſipation and Folly, to which ſhe had recourſe, till the Father of Mercies by his good Spirit, effectually reach'd her when in the full Career of Mirth, being at a publick Evening Entertainment of the neighbouring Youth, about the fifteenth Year of her Age: This ſtrong and humbling Viſitation as ſhe often expreſſed, brought her to ſee the Folly of ſuch Mirth and Jollity, being at that Time attended with ſuch an awful Dread on her Mind, as made her willing to depart from

theſe

thefe vain Amufements, having no longer
Pleafure in them.

She now began to fee the Situation fhe was
in, and the Need fhe had of faving Help,
by which a fecret Hunger and Thirft were
begot in her after Divine and fubftantial
Food, which led her with Diligence to attend
the Way of Worfhip in which fhe had been
educated ; but finding no true Satisfaction
nor proper Nourifhment for her difconfolate
panting Soul, fhe often return'd from the
Place of Worfhip in Tears and great Anxiety
of Mind. She then went among the *Baptifts*,
in Hopes of meeting with what fhe fo ar-
dently defired after ; but being here alfo
difappointed, fhe was led to attend Friends
Meetings, though till now fhe even abhorred
the Name, yet at length through divers clofe
Conflicts and Probations fhe came to experience that Divine Comfort and Confolation
which her Soul had fo longed for and labour'd
after ; the Way of Life and Salvation being
then pointed out to her, fhe had foon to tell
to others what the Lord had done for her
Soul, for about the feventeenth Year of her
Age fhe came forth in a publick Teftimony,
and being faithful and diligent in the Exercife of her Gift fhe became an able Minifter
of the Word, being freely given up to her
great Mafter's Service, thorgh often under

I   great

great temporal Inconveniencies, as her Husband was never poſſeſſed of much of this World, yet their Houſe and Hearts were open to entertain their Friends with the beſt they had ; and it was often Cauſe of humble Thankfulneſs to her Mind, that notwithſtanding their low Beginning they never wanted what was needful, ever preferring the Welfare of Zion before her chiefeſt Joy.

She viſited ſeveral Times moſt Parts of this Nation, *Scotland* and *Ireland,* in which her Services were acceptable, and left laſting Impreſſions on many Minds ; her Miniſtry being in the Demonſtration of Truth, and in the Power thereof. She was fervent in Prayer, being often favour'd with a near Acceſs to the Throne of Grace, to the baptizing of the Aſſemblies into an awful Adoration of him who lives for ever.

Thus through a Variety of Services ſhe laboured faithfully, as well in the Diſcipline as Miniſtry, ſo that a Memorial of her Labours has left a ſweet Savour behind. In private Life, exemplary in Conduct, and in the near Relation of Wife and Mother ; in Converſation innocently chearful, yet ſolid and ſavoury, which rendred her Company very acceptable.

For

For fome Weeks before her Death fhe was confined to her Bed, under fuch bodily Affliction that fhe had not Strength to fay much further than fignifying her Satisfaction at feeing Friends, and her Unity with them : At one Time fhe faid to a Friend who vifited her, *That fhe was very weak in Body, but the Lord was ftrong*; adding, *that fhe was eafy and had Peace of Mind, her Day's Work being done.* There is no Doubt but fhe has laid down her Head in Peace.

She departed this Life the 3d of the Third Month 1762, aged fixty-nine Years, and was interred the 7th of the fame, in Friends Burial-ground in *Lotherfdale* aforefaid.

JOHN RANSOME, of *North-walfham* in the County of *Norfolk*, having been in his Time a lively Example of true Piety, and through a Courfe of a pretty many Years labour'd for its Promotion ; and which he continued till Ilnefs deprived him of his Faculties, and by which Means we are deprived of any Expreffions from him in his laft Ilnefs.

That fuch an Example fhould not be loft, as an Incitement to future Generations to fill

up

up every Duty, and be truly ferviceable alfo in their Day, the following Abftract of a Teftimony from the Quarterly-meeting of *Norfolk* concerning him, is here inferted, *viz.*

" He was educated in the Profeffion of
" Truth, and in his young and tender
" Years reached by the Extendings of
" Divine Love, and happily clofing in
" therewith, he foon gave ample Proofs
" of its Efficacy, that as he grew in Years,
" he grew in the Knowledge and Obedience
" of Truth.

" He came forth in the Miniftry about
" the twenty-eighth Year of his Age ;
" many were the precious Gifts beftowed
" upon him, and the Teftimony given him
" to bear was truly comfortable ; his Open-
" ings deep and inftructive, and he be-
" came an Inftrument of fingular Benefit
" to many, from a true Senfe that was
" given him of their States and Con-
" ditions.

" As an Elder and Overfeer he was
" without Rebuke, his Mind being filled
" with unbounded Charity and Love,
" Counfel and Reproof were well received
" from him ; and as he felt deeply for the
" Infirmities

" Infirmities of all, so he exposed the Fail-
" ings of none. Thus eminently cover'd
" with the Spirit of Healing, he seldom
" met with an Obstinacy able to withstand
" it. He never design'd Offence to any,
" and if through Misapprehension it was
" conceived, he was unwearied in his Ap-
" plication to remove it ; strong in the
" Truth, yet for the Sake of it, subject to
" the Weakest ; suffering all Things, and
" in Condescention sacrificing every selfish
" Consideration to their Help. He loved
" Mankind in Truth, and thus qualified,
" he became a Pattern in Word and Conver-
" sation, adorning the Gospel he preach'd.
" He was endued with a large Share of
" natural Understanding, which being sanc-
" tified by the great and good Hand that
" blessed him with it, rendred him very
" successful in putting an End to Differences
" among his Neighbours and Friends.

" And in the nearest Connections of Life
" he was equally exemplary, being a tender
" loving Husband, an indulgent Parent, an
" affectionate Relation, and strictly regard-
" ful of every Duty towards his Servants,
" his Care over whom was attended with
" singular good Consequences : In these and
" many other Respects, the Loss of him is
" sensibly

" fenfibly felt by us; but we firmly believe
" it is his eternal Gain.

" His Services in the wholfom and necef-
" fary Difcipline eftablifhed in our Society
" were very great, both in Monthly and
" Quarterly-meetings.———And as he was
" exceeding induftrious in what he believed
" to be his Duty, fo was he likewife in
" vifiting the Churches; devoting much of
" his Time and outward Subftance to that
" Service, more particularly in the laft ten
" or twelve Years of his Life.

" He conftantly attended the Service of
" the Yearly-meeting in *London* for many
" Years; the laft Time of his being there
" he was feized with that Ilnefs which con-
" cluded his natural Life; notwithftanding
" his Indifpofition, he vifited feveral large
" Meetings in *Hertfordfhire, Effex* and *Suf-*
" *folk.* He got to his own Dwelling-houfe
" at *Northwalfham* the 20th of the Sixth
" Month, and departed this Life the 2d of
" the Seventh Month 1762, in the fifty-
" fecond Year of his Age.

" His Body was interred on the 6th of the
" fame, in Friends Burial-ground there; a
" very large Concourfe of Friends and others,
" attending the folemn Occafion."

A G N E S

AGNES HALL, Daughter of *William* and *Dorothy Kidd*, of *Settle* in the County of *York*, gave early Tokens of a religious Inclination and filial Affection ; being very ferviceable in her Youth to her infirm Mother, during her Widowhood, in bringing up a pretty numerous Family of Children, fhe being the Eldeft, her Father dying when fhe was about feventeen. Her Conduct may be truly faid to be exemplary in Plainnefs, Moderation and Induftry ; in Benevolence and unaffected Piety ; being of a meek and quiet Difpofition, her Words few and favory, which made her Company truly valuable.

About the thirty-feventh Year of her Age, fhe had to preach the Glad-tidings of the Gofpel, though not large or frequent for fome Years, yet was feafonable, fweet and edifying, much tending to encourage the Youth to give up the Prime of Life to the Service of Truth ; having to acknowledge her Thankfulnefs to the Almighty, that he had wrought a Willingnefs in her Heart in her early Days to bow to his Yoke, which fhe found by bleffed Experience to be eafy, and his Burthen light.

She

She never travelled much in the Work of the Ministry; but was a diligent Attender of Meetings near Home, and very serviceable in the Management of the Affairs of the Church.

Her Indisposition of Body rendred her unable to get to Meetings for a Year before she died: When Friends visited her, tho' she lamented her lonely Situation, and being deprived of getting to Meetings, yet she had at Times to rejoice that she felt the great I AM to be near; he that had been the Stay of her Youth, to be a Staff to lean upon in old Age, and to bear her up with Patience, under great Affliction of Body, in a lively Hope and Assurance of a Resting-place amongst the Righteous.

A Friend visiting her a little before her Death, she was much affected with a Sense of the great Declension in the Church, and of many Superfluities that were crept in, which our ancient Friends had to take up their Cross unto, and bear their Testimony against, the Thoughts whereof much discouraged her; being convinced our Principle remain'd the same, and that we had no nearer Way now to the Fold of Rest than they had.

About

About an Hour before her Death, several Friends visiting her, she being set up in Bed, in a lively Frame of Mind, expressed her great Satisfaction in their Company, *That she sensibly witnessed the Good-will of her heavenly Father to be near, which she had valued all her Life long*; under the Influence whereof she rejoiced and was comforted, and was strongly engaged on the Youth's Account (some young Friends being present) *That they might chuse Truth for their Portion, and* Jacob's *God for the Lot of their Inheritance, which far exceeded every Thing this transitory World would afford*; *and was sorry she had not had more frequent Opportunities of their Company while she had Strength to express her Warmth of Desire for their Growth in the best Things, that would stand them in stead when every Thing else would fail*: And when they took their Leave, she said, *She was glad of that Opportunity, and if she never saw them more, she hoped they should meet in a better Place.*

She was soon after got up in a Chair, where in a few Minutes she quietly departed this Life on the 1st of the Eighth Month 1762. Aged seventy-six Years. And was decently interred in Friends Burial-ground at *Settle* the 4th of the same.

K SARAH

SARAH MARSDEN, Wife of Caleb Marsden, of *Highflatts*, within the Compass of *Pontefract* Monthly - meeting, was born in the Year 1706, and being favour'd with a religious Education, and the Visitations of Truth in her young Years, by yielding Obedience thereto she became a sober, grave. discreet young Woman, a diligent Attender of Meetings, and honestly labouring to improve her Time therein.

About the Year 1749, it pleased the Lord to call her into the Work of the Ministry, which she in great Fear and Tenderness gave up to; and altho' never large in Testimony, yet she was plain, sound and edifying, rather backward in her publick Appearances, and *afraid* (as she said) *to awake her Beloved till he pleased* ; but when she felt the holy Fire burn, then she offer'd her Gift, and was careful when that abated to sit down in Meetings, where too many are intent on Words ; she was a diligent Labourer in Spirit, her very Countenance being awful and affecting, and like the worthy Elders and Nobles of the People, *Numb.* xxi. 18. digging as with the Staff the Lord had given her, and sometimes broke

broke forth in solemn Supplication to the great Law-giver, that the Well of Life might spring up, which at Times she was the happy Instrument of effecting to the Consolation of the Right-minded.

She was naturally of an affable, peaceable Disposition, an affectionate Wife, a tender Mother, and weightily concerned to train up her Children in the Nurture and Admonition of the Lord ; kind to her Friends, charitable to the Poor, and an Example of Humility, Self-denial and Resignation to the Divine Will, and also of Industry and a prudent Management of the Affairs of this Life.

Her last Illness was long and tedious, which she endured with much Patience and Resignation ; saying, *My Body is full of Pain, yea, more than I can well bear ; O the sad State of those in my weak Condition, who want Peace of Mind ! But for ever blessed be my God, who now on my sick Bed answers the Desire of my Mind, in giving me an Evidence of my Peace with him, having nothing to do but to bear with Patience the painful Afflictions that are permitted to attend me ; I find it Work enough to struggle with Nature, one had need have nothing else to do. My Breathing and Travail of Soul hath often been to the Lord that he would let me see my Duty and give me*

K 2   *Strength*

Strength to perform it. If I had my Time to spend over again, I know not that I could spend it much better; I can truly say, I have never been too forward in my Appearances in Meetings, and other Things relating to the Society; but always in great Fear, which sometimes hath been so great that I have been too backward and hurt myself thereby.

To some Friends present, she said, *Dear Friends, stand in your Lots, fear not Man, come up in your proper Places, and the God of Peace will be with you, and strengthen you to perform and come up in the Way of your Duty to him, and one unto another; and so you will be preserved in the pure Love and Unity of the one Spirit.*

At another Time a Friend called to see her, to whom she said, *Thou and I have been very near one unto another, O my Body is full of Pain! I am sometimes ready to say, Lord! What have I done? I want to be eased and dissolved: My Stay here seems very long, at Morning I wish for Night, at Night I long for Morning; but yet blessed be my God, I feel his Hand is underneath, and he bears up my Spirit, or I could not tell how to endure my Affliction.*

At

At another Time, being very weak, she said to her Husband and Children, *At the Time of my Departure be as still as you can, and feel for yourselves, and do not mourn to excess, for all will be well: Do not mourn for me; but rather rejoice when I am delivered from these Pains, for my Change will be a happy one.*

One Evening lying very still, those that attended her thought she had been going to depart; but after some Time she opened her Eyes, and seeing her Relations standing by her, she raised her Voice in a surprizing Manner, and said, *I am intirely sensible, and behold you every one, and glad I am to depart in Peace;* and took her solemn Farewel of all present, in a very loving, affecting and chearful Manner, those present thinking the Time of her Departure had been very near; but she continued some Days longer, mostly lying in a still, quiet, peaceable and resigned Frame of Mind, patiently waiting her Dissolution; and near her Conclusion, her Voice being very weak, she was heard to say, *O that my sweet Redeemer would come and take me to himself! Do not hold me, let me go freely.*

She died the 8th of the Eighth Month 1762, and was interred in Friends Burial-ground

ground at *High-flatts,* the 11th of the same. Aged fifty-six Years.

SAMUEL WATSON, of *Killcon-ner* in the County of *Carlow* in *Ireland,* having been a bright and lively Pattern of true Religion and Virtue; in order that such an Example should not be lost, the following Testimony given forth concerning him is thought meet to be inserted in this Collection, *viz.*

" Our dear and well esteemed Friend
" *Samuel Watson,* of *Killconner* in the County
" of *Carlow* in *Ireland,* succeeded his worthy
" and honourable Father *John Watson,* of
" the same Place, not only in his outward
" Possessions there, but in a zealous Concern
" for the Testimony of Truth, and Support
" of its Cause. Blest with the great Ad-
" vantage of a religious Education, and
" made livingly sensible in his Childhood of
" the precious Influence of Divine Goodness
" extended to his Soul, he grew up in
" Sobriety, Circumspection, and in the Fa-
" vour of God and good Men, being
" preserved through the dangerous Path of
" Youth from the Evils that are in the
" World. When a young Man and intro-
" duced

" duced into Meetings of Difcipline, great
" was the Holy Fear that attended his Mind
" therein, and his ardent Defire was that he
" might never fay or do any thing againft
" the Caufe of Truth ; and as this Fear was
" happily kept to, he not only found it to
" be a Fountain of Life to preferve him
" from the Snares of Death, but experienced
" it to initiate him into the Rudiments of
" true Wifdom, by which in Procefs of
" Time he had Skill to rule well in the
" Houfe of God. Qualified and influenced
" by this Wifdom, he was not only of fin-
" gular Service in the Monthly-meeting to
" which he belonged, but of eminent and
" memorable Ufe in the more general
" Meetings of Bufinefs (which while of
" Ability of Body he attended with exem-
" plary Diligence) in this Nation ; and was
" alfo much efteemed and well received by
" Friends in *England* in his Vifits there :
" For it had pleafed the Lord to endue him
" in a good Meafure with the Gifts and
" Qualifications of an Elder in his Houfe,
" and a Father in the Family. Often
" under the frefh Influence of the Divine
" Anointing, he was enabled to drop living
" Counfel, to the affecting and tendring of
" many Hearts, and to raife that Life in
" Meetings of Difcipline which alone is the
" Crown of all our religious Affemblies.
" Though

" Though sharp in Reproof to those in
" general who trampled upon the Testimony
" of Truth, or lived in a carnal Security,
" yet he greatly rejoiced to see the Buddings
" forth of good Desires in any of the Youth,
" and was a tender nursing Father to such;
" yea, strong and fervent were his Desires
" that the Youth amongst us, and parti-
" cularly his own Children and their Off-
" spring, might dedicate their Hearts fully
" to the Service of God, that there might
" be a Succession of faithful Members in
" the Church whereof Christ is the Head,
" following the Ancients in that self-denying
" Path which they had walked in : At
" Times observing, *That when Friends lived*
" *more retired and inward, the Revelation of*
" *the Spirit and Divine Help was witnessed in*
" *a larger Degree ;* often desiring in his
" declining Years, when his natural Strength
" and Faculties gradually decayed, *That he*
" *might never survive the inward Sense and*
" *Feeling of that which is the Life of the Soul :*
" Also sorrowfully remarking, *That some*
" *by grasping at the present visible Enjoyments,*
" *had left large Possessions to their Families ;*
" *but their Table had become a Snare, and to*
" *several there was left neither Name nor*
" *Memorial amongst us.*

" In

" In religious Vifits to the Families of
" Friends, he was often eminently favoured
" and opened in fuitable Counfel, in an ex-
" traordinary Manner ; and indeed not only
" on thefe appointed Occafions, but in more
" private Conference with thofe of his Fa-
" mily and his Friends : It was apparent he
" dwelt near'the Fountain of Divine Sweet-
" nefs, for Words of fweet Savour, Edifi-
" cation and Tendernefs would often at fuch
" Times flow from him.

" To conclude, he was a careful affecti-
" onate Father, Hufband and Friend, help-
" ful in a civil as well as a religious Capacity
" amongft his Neighbours, and charitable
" to the Poor.

" He departed this Life in Peace, at his
" own Houfe in *Killconner*, the 14th of the
" Fifth Month 1762, and was interred in
" Friends Burying-ground at *Bally-trumbill*,
" in the County of *Carlow* aforefaid, the
" 17th of the fame. Aged feventy-fix
" Years."

GRACE CHAMBERS, an ancient and honourable Friend, of *Kendall* in *Weſtmoreland*, was born at *Munckhelſden* in the County of *Durham*, and while young was virtuouſly inclined, and when ſhe grew up was of a ſtrict exemplary Life and Converſation, remarkable for her Plainneſs and Simplicity of Apparel, Manners and Deportment, endowed with a good Underſtanding and benevolent Diſpoſition, and exerted herſelf to the utmoſt of her Power to be ſerviceable in her Day, which gained her an extenſive Acquaintance among Friends and others, having occaſionally free Acceſs to ſeveral Families of Diſtinction in her Neighbourhood, to whom her affectionate Viſits were acceptable and of Service, and from whom ſhe met with that civil and courteous Behaviour which was due to One of her amiable Qualities.

She had conſiderable Skill in Surgery and in adminiſtring Relief in many Diſorders, which ſhe did without Fee or Reward, and was much devoted to viſit the Sick and thoſe under Affliction, to whom ſhe was greatly helpful. Her Openneſs and Generoſity rofity to her Friends, and Hofpitality to the Poor, were very remarkable.

In the Clofe of her Time fhe was ftrong and lively in her Teftimony, even when bodily Strength was fo much abated, that it was with Difficulty fhe got out to Meetings ; but having been exemplary in this and other Refpects, fhe continued fo to the laft.

Being far advanced in Years, and attended with the Infirmities incident to old Age, fhe bore all with *Chriftian* Patience and Refignation to the alwife difpofing Hand, and finifhed a well-fpent Life, accompanied with the Evidence of a future Well-being, at her Houfe at *Sedgwick* near *Kendall*, the 22d of the Ninth Month 1762, and was decently interred in Friends Burial-ground at *Prefton-Patrick* (the Meeting fhe belonged to) the 26th of the fame. Aged eighty-five Years.

ALICE HALL, Wife of *Isaac Hall*, of *Little-Broughton* in *Cumberland*, was born the 30th of the Eleventh Month 1708, at *Blackhouse* in *Allendale* in *Northumberland*, and Daughter of *John* and *Isabella Fetherstone*, who being religious Friends, carefully educated their Children in the Principles of Truth ; she was early favour'd with Divine Visitations, and being obedient thereto, grew in religious Experience to a good Degree of Stability and Settlement therein ; and having receiv'd a Gift in the Ministry, through an humble Attention to the Leading of the good Shepherd, she became skilful and serviceable in the Church, and freely gave up to that Service, as she found her Mind engaged and drawn thereto.

In her unmarried State she was concern'd to visit Friends twice in *Ireland*, most Parts of *England*, *Wales* and *Scotland* ; was both a good Example in private Life, and in her publick Ministry, abiding under the seasoning Virtue, which rendred her Conversation edifying and agreeable. After her Marriage, which was in the Year 1742, she remain'd zealous for the Cause of Truth, and was

often

often concerned to travel in the Service thereof, vifiting feveral Parts of her native Land, and *Ireland* a third Time.

In the Year 1760 fhe found an Engagement to vifit the Churches in *America*, which proved a very clofe Trial, in parting from her Hufband and Children ; but after recommending them to the Protection of that Hand which is for ever fufficient, fhe proceeded on her Voyage, and landed in *America* in the Tenth Month 1761, and diligently fet about her Services, vifiting the Provinces generally, altho' weak in Body, in Company of a Friend of *Pennfilvania*, named *Ann Newland* ; and her Labours of Love through the different Provinces were to the general Satisfaction of Friends, as appears by divers Certificates tranfmitted from thence.

She was alfo enabled to vifit many Meetings in the Provinces of *Pennfilvania* and the *Jerfeys*, altho' under great bodily Weaknefs and great Exercife of Spirit ; yet her meek, lowly and innocent Deportment, together with her lively and edifying Miniftry, made lafting Impreffions on many Minds, and rendred her Company very acceptable.

In the Courfe of her vifit, fhe was an Example of great Patience and Humility, steady

steady in Attention to her own Bufinefs, and prudent in Converfation, difcharging her Duty faithfully in her weighty Undertaking.

A little before fhe was confined by Ilnefs, fhe expreffed to fome Friends after the laft publick Meeting fhe was able to attend, which was at *Chefter* in *New-Jerfey, That fhe was clear*; and altho' the Yearly-meeting at *Philadelphia* was then to be held in a few Days, fhe faid, *She could not fee fhe fhould be at it.*

She got to her Lodging at *Ifaac Zane*'s in *Philadelphia*, the 22d of the Ninth Month 1762, and her Diftemper increafing, notwithftanding all the tender Care Affection could dictate, fhe expired the 6th of the Tenth Month following. She endured her laft Ilnefs, which was very fharp, without any Signs of murmuring, but in Lamb-like Patience expreffed an entire Refignation in the Divine Will, whether to live or die.

Her Body was carried to one of the Meeting-houfes in *Philadelphia*, and after a large and folemn Meeting was decently interred in Friends Burial-ground in the City, the 8th of the Tenth Month 1762.

BOSSALL

BOSSALL MIDDLETON, of *Boroughbridge* in the County of *York*, having thro' a long Courfe of Years maintain'd a fteady Teftimony in Oppofition to all undue Liberties, and labour'd for the Promotion of Truth, which he was enabled to do thro' Divine Experience and Obedience to the Heavenly Light ; and though through extream old Age, his Memory became impair'd for the laft two or three Years of his Life, yet a fhort Account of him for the Encouragement of fuch as may hereafter read this, claims a Place in thefe Memoirs.

He was a diligent Attender of Meetings, and peculiarly qualified for the Support of Difcipline, awfully waiting 'for the Arifing of that Divine Power, which is unerring, to direct his Judgment.

He twice fuffer'd Imprifonment by a Prieft for the Non-payment of his Demands, about eleven Years, which he bore with much *Chriftian* Patience and Refignation, being exemplary in Suffering, and was fo attended by Divine Affiftance, that he fervently defired his Adverfary might be forgiven.

About

About the feventieth Year of his Age, his Mouth was opened in publick Teftimony, which was found, refrefhing and edifying, greatly to the Satisfaction of the Right-minded ; and as he bought the Truth he was careful not to fell it, fo it may be juftly faid, Truth and its Friends were his beloved Companions, and his Conduct among Men gain'd him Love and Efteem.

To fome Friends who vifited him a little before his Deceafe, he appeared to be in a ftill, quiet, fweet, compofed Frame of Mind, and took his laft Leave of them in his ufual tender and affectionate Manner.

Much might be faid of this worthy Friend ; but as his Life was a Series of clofe Exercifes and Trials, it may fuffice to fay, he endured them as a Man whofe Mind was wean'd from the World, having his Eye fixed on a far better Country, namely an Heavenly, into which there is no Doubt of his being entered.

He departed this Life the 8th of the Fifth Month 1763, in the ninety-fixth Year of his Age, and a Minifter about twenty-feven Years, and was buried at *Burton* near *Barnfley* the 10th of the fame.

JOHN

JOHN GOODWIN, an ancient Friend at *Efkyrgoch* in *Montgomeryfhire* in *North-Wales,* was early favour'd with the bleffed Vifitation of Truth, and by faithfully adhering to the Dictates thereof, he experienced its Effects to be redeeming him, and purifying him as a Veffel for the great Mafter's Ufe ; fo that about the twenty-feventh Year of his Age, he was called to the Work of the Miniftry, in which through faithfully and diligently waiting for all-fufficient Help, he became an able Minifter of the Gofpel, and was inftrumental to turn many from Darknefs to Light, and from the Power of Satan to the Power of God, that he might well be number'd among the Valiants of *Ifrael* ; often vifiting the Principality of *Wales,* and in his younger Part of his Life, divers Parts of *England* : He filled up the feveral Duties of Life with good Repute, being an affectionate Hufband, a tender Father, a good Neighbour : Alfo in a religious Senfe, a wife nurfing Father, pleafant in Converfation, yet weighty and inftructive to thofe who enquired the Way to Sion ; when led to reprove, he was careful to abide in the Spirit of Meeknefs and Wifdom. He was of an upright Life and Converfation, a

M   fervent

fervent Lover of the Cause of Truth and People of God, zealous of the Honour of Truth and the Support of its Testimony in all its Branches.

In his younger Years, when in low Circumstances, and anxious for the Support of his Family, he purposed removing to *America* (his Parents, Brother and Sisters being gone thither before) but finding a Stop in his Mind, and feeling after Divine Counsel, he found it his Place to settle in his native Land, and it livingly arose in his Heart *that the Lord would provide for him and his Family*, in which he believed ; and in the Close of his Days said with Thankfulness, *The Lord had fulfilled it to him* ; which is worthy of Commemoration, and may serve as a Way-mark to others who read this Account, to have their Eye to him in Faith, with whom Counsel dwells, for Direction in all their Concerns of Life.

He continued fresh and lively to old Age; and about three Weeks before his Decease, at the last publick Meeting he attended, he was enabled to bear Testimony in the Life and Power of Truth, in a remarkable Manner, to those present, amongst whom were divers not in Society with us ; and after Meeting said, *He was fully clear of the People,*

People, and releafed from that Service ; figni-
fying his Time here was near a Conclufion,
and that now after a painful Affliction he
fhould foon be at Reft with the Righteous, for
which he long'd ; yet faid, Let Patience have
its perfect Work.

During his Ilnefs he appeared to be in an
Heavenly Frame of Mind, abounding with
Praifes to God for his continued Mercies,
often expreffing how valuable the Enjoyment of the Love of God is on a Dying-
bed. He defired his Love might be remembred to his Brethren and Sifters in
Chrift, being fenfible and clear in his Underftanding to the laft Hour.

He quietly departed this Life, as one
falling into a fweet Sleep, the 7th of the
Twelfth Month 1763, and was buried in
Friends Burial-ground at *Llwyndee,* the 12th
of the fame. Aged about eighty-two Years.

CATHA-

CATHARINE BURLING, Daughter of *John* and *Ann Burling*, of the City of *New-York* in *America*, was taken ill of a flow *Fever*, which weaken'd her gradually, so that (to ufe her own Expreffions) fhe was *reduced ſtep by ſtep*, all Means ufed for her Help proving ineffectual.

When fhe was brought low and her Recovery appear'd doubtful, fhe was for a Time under great Exercife of Mind concerning her future State, and prayed to the Lord for a little more Time, and that fhe might witnefs a better State; which he was gracioufly pleafed to anfwer, not long after faying, *Her Mind was changed.* She came to witnefs the Child's State, filled with Innocency, abounding in Love; often faying, *My Mind is like a little Child's*; and her Heart came to be filled with the Love of God, and in the Aboundings thereof, for feveral Weeks before her Departure, fhe was at Times enabled to declare of the Lord's Goodnefs to her in a wonderful Manner; and alfo, to exhort many who came to vifit her, to *Amendment of Life, that when they came to lie on a ſick Bed they might be made Enjoyers of that Peace ſhe was then*
made

made a Partaker of ; often saying, *She felt his Peace flow in her Mind as a gentle Stream, and that her Cup run over.*

Though Order of Time may not be kept ſtrictly to, yet many were the ſweet Expreſſions which this young Woman uttered, ſome of which, as near as could be remembred, are as follows, *viz.*

Many weariſome Nights have I gone thro', and have watered my Pillow with my Tears. I was long in Doubt of my eternal Happineſs, and in the Time of greateſt Diſtreſs, I cried to the Lord that he would be pleaſed to lengthen my Time a little longer that I might be more fully prepared, and he was graciouſly pleaſed to hear and grant my Requeſt ; and now he has been pleaſed to grant me a full Aſſurance of it, and to lengthen my Time, that I might ſpeak of his Goodneſs to others, and tell what he has done for my Soul ; O Praiſes, Praiſes, Praiſes, be given to his great and glorious Name ! My Tongue is too ſhort by far, O if I had the Tongue of an Angel, I could not ſufficiently expreſs my Gratitude to that gracious God who has been thus pleaſed to favour me in ſo eminent a Manner !

My Diſorder is very changeable, very flattering it would be to ſome, but it does not flatter

flatter me; I am refign'd to the Lord's Will, let him do juſt as beſt pleaſeth him with me, his poor frail Creature. A few Days ago, when I thought I was juſt launching into Eternity, that boundleſs Ocean of Eternity, I prayed to the Lord that he would be pleaſed to give me a little longer Time, and he was graciouſly pleaſed to hear and grant my Requeſt. The Work of Regeneration is a great Work, I know it now experimentally, I am become a new Creature, new Thoughts, new Deſires, my Affections ſet upon Things above; I have a new Name written in the Lamb's Book of Life, and the white Stone is given to me.

She at the ſame Time adviſed her Brothers and Siſters to Plainneſs of Speech and Apparel, ſaying, Remember our bleſſed Lord, that great Pattern of Plainneſs, who when on Earth went up and down doing Good, and wore a Garment without Seam : He was crucified, he was nailed to the Croſs for our Sins, for my Sins : O Love inexpreſſible !

During the laſt five Weeks of her Ilneſs, ſhe was frequently ſpeaking of the Lord's Goodneſs to her, ſhe being favour'd in an extraordinary Manner ; often ſaying, I have nothing to do with this World, O let my Time be employ'd in praiſing the Lord, and telling of his gracious Dealings with my Soul !

One

One Evening her Father was sitting by her Bed-side, she said to him, *Thou art my Father, but now I have another Father, I have an Heavenly Father ; I love thee dearly, but I love him much more, O he is the Chiefest of ten Thousands !*

. She would often say, *I am thankful to the Lord for all his Favours conferred on me, and when I don't speak I am thankful in my Heart, and that is more than Words ; the Lord don't require. Lip-honour, but when my Heart is filled I can't help speaking.*

At another Time, *Many are the Changes and Vicissitudes I do experience, and what may come next there are none of us knows ; but I am resign'd and thankful for all his Mercies, his poor frail Creature : He must do with me just as he pleases ; we should be thankful for all the Lord's Favours. I hope and pray that I may be kept thankful and humble, meek and low, before him, waiting for my Change, and a happy Change it will be to me.*

One Morning as her Mother and Sisters were putting on her Cloaths, she desired them to stop, and then expressed herself to this Effect : *I now no longer wonder that the Martyrs could sing in the Flames, I could do the same ; I think I could go through burning Flames,*

Flames, if required, for the Love of Chrift,
O it is inexpreffible ! And fpake mucli
more, and then prayed in an extraordinary
Manner.

At another Time fhe fpoke to the Purpofe
following : *Now I know how precious the*
Soul is, O that People would prize their Time,
and prepare while Health is granted them !
I blefs the Lord I am prepared, if he is pleafed
to call me the next Moment, I am ready ; but
I am thankful for the little Time he has
granted me to be with you : But, O how
fhocking, how horribly fhocking muft it be for
fuch poor Souls who are unprepared and de-
prived of their Senfes at fuch a Time as this !

She often exhorted and advifed many
young People, at different Times, againft
reading Romances and idle Books, faying,
It has been the greateft Trouble and Exercife
of Mind to me, more than any thing I have
done, it has coft me many a wearifome Night
and many a bitter Tear, though I have never
read but a few, and thofe that were deem'd
the moft harmlefs ; I know there are fome
who deem them innocent Amufements, and
fay, Thofe Books are inftruEtive and there are
good Morals in them : But, O muft we go to
fuch Books for good Morals ! Read the Scrip-
tures,

*tures, which are the best of all Books, and
there are other good Books.*

One following the Sea coming into the
Room, and standing by her Bed-side, after
a few Minutes she spoke to him to this
Import : *Thou art one that saileth on the
great Waters, and there thou may see God's
Wonders in the great Deeps ; and thou art
much in Company with Sailors and such like
Men, and I know they are light and frothy
in their Conversation ; and I desire thee to
keep thy Mind watchful and near the Lord,
which if thou doest, thou wilt be preserved in
his Fear.*

When she mended after a severe Turn of
Ilness, one Evening she called her little
Brothers to her, and kissed them in a very
loving Manner; and then being removed to
the Bed-side, as she sat thereon she said,
*O I am full of Love! I feel a Degree of
Divine Love.* A Neighbour being in the
Room, noticing how easy and composed her
Countenance was, she answer'd, *How can
my Countenance be sad when my Mind is at
Peace ;* the Neighbour answering, *Which
the World cannot give,* she return'd, *No nor
take away.*

Two

Two Neighbours not of our Society coming into the Room, she spoke to one of them, saying, *Thou sees me very weak and low, but my Mind is at Peace, sweet Heavenly Peace of Mind; I hope and pray that thou may feel the same when thou comes to lie on a sick Bed.*

Through the Prevalence of her Distemper and for Want of Sleep, she became delirious for some Days, with small Intermissions; and then at such Intervals she seem'd filled with Divine Love. The last Day before her Departure, she bid her Sister tell her Mother, *I am resign'd, patiently waiting and quietly hoping for my happy Change.* A little before her Departure, she told her Father, *She was not afraid to die:* Soon after she said to one of her Sisters, *I feel as if I am going to Paradise.* About Noon the same Day, she desired her Mother to tell a Friend present, *That she should go easy and to Rest.*

She departed this Life without Sigh or Groan, the 16th of the Fourth Month 1764, between the Hours of eight and nine in the Evening, in the eighteenth Year of her Age, and was decently interred in Friends Burying-ground in *New-York.*

JOHN

JOHN ALDERSON, of *Ra-venstondale* in *Westmoreland*, was the Son of our ancient Friends *Ralph* and *Alice Alderson*, of the same Place, and was educated by them in a religious Manner, who both by Example and Precept, were signally serviceable to him in the Time of his Youth, to whom he demean'd himself, as he became truly religious, in a very dutiful Manner.

About the nineteenth Year of his Age, he was remarkably favoured with an humbling Visitation from on High, which as he kept under, he became fitted for the Work of the Ministry, into which he was called about twelve Years aftewards; wherein in a short Time he grew skilful, and labour'd with unwearied Diligence, visiting divers Parts of this Nation several Times : He also visited *Ireland* and *Scotland*; in all which there is good Reason to believe his Labours were acceptable, and of good Service to the Churches. In Time of Silence, he was close and steady in a fervent Travail of Spirit before the Lord ; was often enabled to unfold the deep Mysteries of the Kingdom, and the Work of Regeneration ; and also strongly to press Friends, to a steady Watch-

N 2

fulness

fulnefs againft the many fubtil Wiles and Temptations of the Enemy of Man's Happiness.

In the Beginning of the Year 1764, altho' under great Weakneſs of Body, he found a Concern to pay a religious Viſit to Friends in the Southern Parts of the Nation, and in Company with his beloved Friend *Anthony Maſon*, he came to *London*, but under great Indiſpoſition, being able to attend but a few Meetings in that City, in which he appeared in publick Teſtimony, to the Comfort and Satisfaction of many, particularly in the Meeting of Miniſters and Elders ; but his natural Strength decreaſing, he was confined about ſeventeen Weeks at the Houſe of our Friend *Thomas Jackſon*, where all neceſſary Care and Aſſiſtance were adminiſtred to him.

In the Courſe of his Ilneſs he was led under the Influence of Divine Love, to leave a few Hints reſpecting the Beginning and Progreſs of Truth upon his Soul, and ex- preſſed himſelf to this Effect : " That he " was mercifully viſited with the Day- " ſpring from on High, and in the Light " of the Lord it was clearly diſcovered to " him, *what he ſhould do* and *what he ſhould* " *abſtain from* ; but being addicted to " youthful Follies and Vanities, he was
" unwilling

" unwilling to renounce them, as well as to
" come up in Obedience to the Advice and
" Admonitions of his faithful and expe-
" rienced Parents in the Truth. By his
" Difobedience he *put out the Candle which*
" *the Lord had lighted in his Soul*, and con-
" tinued for fome Time to walk in Dark-
" nefs ; in which dark and wildernefs State,
" the Almighty, for wife Purpofes by him
" unfeen, fuffered Satan to try and prove
" him with *various Temptations* ; not only
" with the Glory of temporal Delights, but
" with Sins exceeding finful in their Nature.
" He had received a Meafure of Light and
" Grace, but he rebelled againft it ; and
" though he was kept from grofs Pollutions,
" yet his vain, light and airy Mind, and
" afpiring Imagination, was unwilling to
" fubmit to the Yoke of Chrift to follow
" him in Humility and Self-denial ; and as
" he had by Tranfgreffion againft the inward
" Law, which is Light, forfeited his Right
" to the Tree of Life, he found no Way
" for a Return but by the flaming Sword,
" which in an eminent Manner feem'd fur-
" bifhed for him in order to divide the
" Precious from the Vile, and which did
" execute the fierce Anger of the Lord upon
" his tranfgreffing Nature, which was ftrong
" and unwilling to have Sin deftroy'd both
" Reot and Branch. For fome Time the
" Lord

" Lord executed his juſt Judgments ſo that
" his Terrors made him afraid that his
" Mercy was clear gone from him for ever,
" which brought him to deſpair of attaining
" Life eternal.

" But when the Almighty (who redeems
" Zion through Judgment) was pleaſed to
" ſay, *It was enough*, and this Diſpenſation
" of Condemnation had humbled his Spirit,
" and bowed his Neck to the Yoke of
" Chriſt, by the powerful Operation of
" whoſe Spirit he became as Clay in the
" Hands of the Potter ; and though the
" Miniſtration of Condemnation had been
" glorious, he could now ſing of *Judgment*
" *and Mercy*. And as he kept faithful to
" the Diſcoveries of the Light which now
" ſhone brighter to the perfect Day, he
" was preſerved therein from turning again
" to Folly ; knowing by purchaſed Expe-
" rience, that all who are ſaved from Sin,
" and perſevere in a Life of Righteouſneſs,
" muſt walk ſteadily in the Light of the
" Lord.

" While he was in the Employment of a
" Shepherd, being alone, he was by the
" Love of God ſo powerfully attracted to
" love him again, and all Mankind, that
" under the Sacred Influence and Holy
                                    " Anointing

" Anointing thereof, he found the Gospel
" of Salvation flowed univerfally towards
" all, and the Word of Life fprang and
" flowed in his Soul as if he had been
" preaching to many People."

Thus this dear Friend became qualified
for the Work of the Miniftry, a Difpenfation of which was given to him, that he
might fhow unto Man the Way of Life and
Salvation.

Much excellent Counfel and Advice alfo
dropt from him, in the Courfe of his Ilnefs,
to Minifters and Elders in their various
States and Allotments, his Underftanding and
Memory being preferved clear and ftrong to
the laft, being alfo bleffed with remarkable
Serenity and Calmnefs in that proving Seafon. Towards the Clofe of his Time, after
commending every one *to God, and to the
Word of his Grace and good Spirit*, he added,
for whofe Sake, fays he, *I have travelled in
the Deeps ; and now in the feeming Conclufion of my Time, I witnefs renewed Peace and
Divine Refrefhment, and with my languifhing
Breath, under the Influence of Gofpel Love,
I am enabled to pray for the Peace of our
Zion, that Truth and Righteoufnefs may profper
within her Gates, and the Salvation of our
God may be yet appointed as Walls and Bul-
warks*

warks about her City. This is what I continue
earnestly to wish, not only for my Brethren
and Fellow-members, but for every one who
may receive the Invitation of God's Love, and
be obedient to the Dictates of his Spirit, and so
become Inhabitants of this Holy City, the City
of the great King, who is ever worthy to rule
and reign in the Hearts of his People : Then
adding, *Thus having relieved my Spirit, there
remains nothing but to desire my endeared Love
may be remembred to my affectionate Wife,
who, says he, I desire may not grieve beyond
measure, but freely resign me into the Hands
of my faithful Creator ; also to my dear
Children, with my dear aged Parents and
Relations according to the Flesh ; telling them,
that through the continued Loving-kindness of
a merciful Saviour, it is well with me, and
I am favoured with a comfortable Evidence,
that if I am removed with the present Weakness of Body, he will receive me into the Arms
of his Mercy ; and that I go to their God,
and my God, to their Father and my Father,
to join the Heavenly Host, in ever magnifying
his Love and Mercy, who hath loved and
washed us in the Blood of the immaculate
Lamb : To whom, with the Father, through
the Holy Spirit, be Glory, Honour and Praise,
now and eternally in the Heavens. Amen.*

He

He departed this Life the 26th of the Fourth Month 1764, about Midnight, and his Body was interred in *Bunhill-fields* the 30th of the fame, after a large and folemn Meeting at *Devonfhire-houfe*, held for that Purpofe. Aged near forty-three, and a Minifter about twelve Years.

See an Account concerning him in Print, intituled, *Some ufeful Obfervations and Advices.*

STEPHEN SEDGEWICK, an ancient Friend belonging to *Bentham* Monthly-meeting in *Yorkfhire*, was born about the Year 1684, and educated in the Way of Truth as profeffed by us, and when very young became concern'd to live a fober and religious Life, frequently feeking folitary Places to pour forth his Soul in Supplication to the Lord, that he might know an inward Acquaintance with him for himfelf; and as he grew in Years he grew in faving Knowledge, fo that about the twentieth Year of his Age his Mouth was open'd in Miniftry, and through Faithfulnefs he became an able Minifter of the Gofpel, having frequently to declare to others what the Lord had done for his Soul, to the Encouragement of the weak and fincere Mind.

O

He

He laboured diligently, and visited most of the Meetings in this Nation, *Scotland* and *Ireland*, and was frequently engaged in visiting the Families of Friends; in which Service he was eminently qualified.

During the latter Part of his Life he was afflicted with bodily Weakness, yet still continued a constant Attender of Meetings, both for Worship and Discipline; and it was clearly observable, the nearer he grew towards his final Change, the more lively and bright he grew in his Gift in the Ministry.

His Life and Conversation was remarkably regular and inoffensive, his Benevolence extended to all, whereby he obtained a good Report and Esteem.

During his last Illness he often declared to those who visited him, *That his Day's Work was done, that he had nothing to do but die, and that he was in true Peace with the Lord and all Men.*

He departed this Life the 10th of the Fifth Month 1764, and was buried in Friends Burial-ground at *Lower-Bentham.* Aged about eighty Years, a Minister sixty Years.

ELIZABETH

ELIZABETH KENDALL, late of *Manningtree* in *Essex*, was convinced of the Truth in her young and tender Years, altho' in the Beginning was not fensible what it was that followed her with Reproofs, if at any Time she missed or turned her Feet out of the Way which she was convinced she should walk in ; which brought great Anguish upon her tender Mind, and made her to seek solitary Places to pour out her Tears before the Lord, who heard her Prayers and Supplications for Prefervation, and was her alone Helper.

Her Parents not being at all fensible of her Trouble of Mind, and that it was for her Soul's Sake, that it might rest in the Day of Trouble, began to be very harsh with her, by Threatning and using all Endeavours to drive her from such Thoughtfulness, fearing it would be her Ruin. But powerful was that good Hand and Arm which was made bare for her Support, so that the more her Suffering encreased the stronger she grew.

At this Time she was quite unacquainted with Friends, not knowing there was such a

O 2   People ;

People ; but some Time after her Parents
removing to a Place near which some Friends
refided, she became acquainted with them,
in whose Company she was often refreshed,
and her afflicted Mind much comforted ;
and hearing of a Meeting she found Means
to get to it, in which (tho' there were but
few Words spoken) she was melted down as
Wax before the Fire, not wanting to hear
Words ; but was sensible these were the
People she was to join with, which she did
for Peace-sake about the nineteenth Year of
her Age. Then did her Sufferings encreafe
by her Parents, but in a more severe Manner
from her Father, he having a great Dislike
to the Name *Quaker*, saying, *I had rather
she had been any thing but that*, and spoke
much against them ; yet was she steady and
immovable, many Times having much to
say in Vindication of the Truth, but he could
not bear it, therefore was more severe against
her.

About the twenty-first Year of her Age,
she came forth in a publick Testimony to the
great Comfort and Satisfaction of Friends,
which occasioned a fresh Trouble to her
Parents, and made her Sufferings still greater
from them ; yet it did not alter her steady
Resolutions in pressing forward in that which
brought

brought Peace, neither occasioned her to shew any Uneasiness to her Parents.

One Day her Father being in great Warmth took her by the Arm and thrust her out at the Door, saying, *Let me never see you more if you do not leave the* Quakers ; she patiently bore it and went to a Friend's House, who gladly received her 'till further Way was opened.

After some Time it pleased the Almighty to grant her Father a Visitation of the Day-spring from on High, which brought him to a Sight of his State and Condition, and made him seek a Place of Repentance : And he became willing to suffer and to endure the Cross, and betook himself to a very circum-spect Way of Life ; and after a considerable Time, hearing his Daughter was to be at a Meeting near where he resided, privately got to it ; in which she was favour'd to bear a living Testimony to the Truth, and was made instrumental to his being fully con-vinced ; after Meeting he embraced her with Tears, saying, *My dear Child, hold on thy Way, fear no Man, thou art in the Right.* And from that Time he constantly went to Meetings, and continued faithful to the End of his Time ; some Time after his Wife,

Wife, one Son and another Daughter joined Friends.

After some Time she settled at *Bradfield* near *Manningtree* in *Essex*, and being freely given up to the Lord's Requirings, grew much in the Truth; her Testimony was large, lively, and powerful, to the great Comfort and Satisfaction of the Honesthearted. She was often concerned to go forth and leave all that was near and dear to her behind; was several Times drawn to visit Friends in this Nation, once in *Ireland*, twice in *Wales* and *Scotland*, and in all was well received; appear'd much to the Consolation of the Afflicted, but as a sharp threshing Instrument to the Careless, and to the stirring up and awakening many.

A Pattern of Plainness and true Humility, zealous for promoting the Truth, having no greater Joy than to see its Professors prosper in it, nor spared any Pains to admonish or rebuke where Occasion required.

For several Years before her Decease she was attended with great bodily Weakness, yet as long as it was possible to be had to Meetings did not give it over; soon after her being disabled from attending Meetings, she was taken with something of the *Palsey*, which

which affected her Speech, so that she could not well express herself, but was sometimes understood to say, *I love, I love all :* Nothing more pleasant to her than to see her Friends. She was often retired in her Mind, Sweetness appearing in her Countenance ; a Pattern of Patience, not finding Fault with what was done for her, nor heard to say, it was hard she should be afflicted with so many Weaknesses ; but always appearing in an easy Frame of Mind with great Pleasantness, endeavouring to make those about her sensible she counted it a great Favour she was so provided for.

She departed this Life the 19th, and was interred the 24th of the Second Month 1765, in Friends Burial-ground at *Manningtree*, about the eightieth Year of her Age, having been a Minister fifty-eight Years.

GHARRETT VAN HASSEN, an ancient Friend of *Dublin*, was born in *Holland*, he was a signal Instance of the Mercy and long Forbearance of a gracious God, having been favour'd with a Divine and powerful Visitation about the fortieth Year of his Age, and thereby reclaim'd from a State of Unregeneracy and Sin, witnessing
true

true Repentance : He join'd in Society with us the People called *Quakers*, and through Faithfulness, being led on in the Paths of Piety and Love to God and Men, he received a Gift in the Miniftry in *England*, and about the Year 1737 he went to *Ireland*, and for the moft Part of the Remainder of his Time refided at *Dublin*.

He was a fervent Labourer in the Miniftry, and zealous in his Teftimony againft the inordinate Love of the World, affectionately tender to the Youth, and was often concerned for their Prefervation.

He vifited the Meetings of Friends in *Great-Britain* ; and in the Year 1747 he performed a Vifit to moft or all the Families of Friends in *Ireland*, and alfo to fuch as had by Mifconduct juftly iucurred the Cenfure of the Society ; in which Labour he was well received, having extenfive Charity.

During the latter Part of his Time, he was greatly afflicted with bodily Infirmities, difabling him in a great meafure for publick Service ; but he ftill retained his Love to God and the Brethren, and at or near his Conclufion had the comfortable Affurance of his approaching Removal to a better State, which he fignified by the following Expreffions

Expreffions among others : *I am going to your Father and my Father; to your God and my God : I die daily, neverthelefs I live, and not I, but Chrift liveth in me.*

He departed this Life the 30th of the Sixth Month 1765. Aged about feventy, a Minifter upwards of twenty-eight Years.

RACHEL CHANDLER, formerly PENFOLD, was born at *Guilford* in the County of *Surry* ; her Mother dying when fhe was young, fubject- ed her to many Inconveniencies, which fhe occafionally mentioned ; but being favoured with an early Vifitation of Divine Love, was preferved from the groffer Pollutions of the Age, and by gradually fubmitting to the fanctifying Operation of Truth, was fitted for the Work of the Miniftry, and diligently labouring to improve the Talent committed to her Truft, in due Time became an able Minifter of the Gofpel, found in Doctrine, rightly dividing the Word of Truth. She travelled thro' divers Parts of this Nation in full Unity with her Friends, and to the Peace and Satisfaction of her own Mind.

Her

Her Miniſtry was attended with a lively Demonſtration of the Spring from whence it flowed ; ſhe was often favour'd with near Acceſs to the Throne of Grace, in fervent Supplication for the Reſtoration of Zion, to her primitive Purity and Beauty ; and in Commemoration of the Lord's Goodneſs to her through the various Diſpenſations of his Providence, would frequently exhort the Youth to *Remember their Creator in the Days of their Youth, and dedicate the Prime of their Days to his Service.*

She was a nurſing Mother to the Tender and Well-inclined, and a true Sympathizer with the Bowed-down and Afflicted in Spirit ; but a ſharp Reprover of the Rebellious and Stiff-necked ; an affectionate Friend and kind Neighbour ; a Pattern of Induſtry, Humility, and Self-denial ; a good Example in diſcharging the ſeveral relative Duties ſuitable to her Station and Circumſtances in Life, which made her beloved both by Friends and others.

She was long afflicted with a ſore Diſorder, which rendred her incapable of Travelling for a conſiderable Time ; but ſhe conſtantly attended her own Meeting, and after, when her Inability encreaſed, the Meeting was held at her Houſe, where ſhe frequently
appear'd

appear'd in publick Testimony, under a living Sense that the Lord had not forsaken her in this Time of outward Affliction.

To her Husband and a Friend who came to see her, she said, *If she died then her Desire was that they would look to their own Standing, and not grieve for her, but rather rejoice she was landed safe from a World of Peril and Difficulty, a Life of Temptation and Probation ; that the last Thing she had to struggle with was Death, and that was made easy, the Sting thereof being taken away.*

At another Time being in great Pain, *O if I had my Peace to make now, what should I do ! It is enough to bear the Infirmities of the Body, without the Load of a guilty Conscience.* Being a little easier, she said, *That her Pain was often very strong, yet at Times she witnessed great Sweetness, which supported and enabled her to bear her Affliction ;* further adding, *A little of the Balm of* Gilead *was very comfortable to her, and that she longed for the Time to come when she might drink large Draughts of Water from the Well of Life.*

She was several Months confined to her Bed, but bore her Affliction with remarkable Patience and Resignation, and continued
sensible

senfible to her End, departing this Life the 18th of the Fifth Month 1765, and was interred in Friends Burial-groud at *Kingston* the 24th of the fame. Aged forty-two, a Minifter fixteen Years.

A few Months before her Death, fhe drew up a brief Memorial of the gracious Dealings of the Lord with her Soul, which fhe defired might be communicated to Friends, and is here annexed.

A brief Memorial of the Lord's gracious Dealings with Rachel Chandler, *formerly* R. Penfold, *late of* Efher *in* Surry, *written by herfelf a few Months before her Deceafe, and at her particular Requeft communicated to Friends.*

" WHEN I confider that the Grave
" cannot celebrate the Praife that is
" due to the Lord, on Account of his
" gracious and merciful Dealings to my
" Soul, I am inclined to fay fo much on
" God's Behalf, as may fuffice to let Man-
" kind know, that he of his own free
" Mercy firft vifited my Soul, when it was
" gone very far aftray from the right Path ;
" and

" and at about the feventeenth Year of
" my Age, laid the Axe to the Root of
" the corrupt Tree, and fhook my fandy
" Foundation, fo that my feeble Building,
" grounded on Profeffion and Name, was
" made to totter, and I to cry out in the
" Anguifh of my Spirit, *What fhall I do*
" *to become what I ought to be, that fo I*
" *might obtain Favour and Peace with God !*
" And fuch was my Sorrow Night and Day,
" that I often wifh'd I had never been born,
" or that I had died very young before I
" had Knowledge of Good and Evil ; for
" now that the Book of the Law was
" open'd, the Commandment came, Sin
" revived that had been hid and cover'd
" with a Fig-leaf Covering, and I died,
" and as one fenfible of the Terrors of the
" Lord, I often cried, *O wretched Creature*
" *that I am ! Who fhall deliver me from*
" *this Body of Sin and Death ?* Thus went
" I fecretly mourning on my Way for a
" long Time, while my Adverfary laid
" many Baits in my Way to catch my
" unwary Feet ; yet when ever I yielded to
" the forcible Power of Conviction, tho'
" in ever fo trivial Things, I found Peace ;
" but as I had gone a great Way from the
" Father's Houfe, fo I had a great Way to
" come back, and it took up much Time,
" for there was long War between the
" Houfe

" House of *Saul* and the House of *David*,
" but bleſſed be God, the Father and Foun-
" tain of Life, the Houſe of *David* grew
" ſtronger as the Houſe of *Saul* grew
" weaker, ſo that in Time my Enemies
" were diſcomfitted, and what I had ſeen
" and heard in ſecret at the Bottom of
" Jordan and in the Depth of the Sea, was
" I requir'd to proclaim as on the Houſe-
" top ; which was ſo weighty an Engage-
" ment that it took up much Time to be
" fitted for, leaſt not being rightly pre-
" pared I ſhould be drawn in a forward
" Zeal to do that which was not required
" of me, as poor *Uzzah* did, or being
" rightly anointed, yet through a forward
" Mind to be doing, ſhould be haſtily drawn
" to offer Sacrifice before *Samuel* came ; ſo
" that after repeated Manifeſtations and
" convincing Circumſtances had been af-
" forded, yet the confirming Evidence be-
" ing wanting, I durſt not appear in publick
" Teſtimony for God, until *Gideon*-like, I
" had tried the Fleece every Way, by which
" the Long-forbearance of the Lord was
" diſcovered to me-ward, who knew my
" with-holding was not from obſtinate Re-
" bellion, but through Fear of taking that
" on me which I was not called to, and
" that my Deſire in doing his Work was
" that I might be his Servant, and found
                                   " anſwering

" anſwering the End for which I was made,
" that rightly improving my Talent, I
" might at laſt have an Entrance into the
" Joy of my Lord : And at length having
" waited the Seaſon for the accompliſhing
" the Work of manifeſting my Love by
" my Obedience, I gave up in great
" Weakneſs and Trembling to ſpeak a few
" Words in Meetings in the twenty-ſixth
" Year of my Age, and had great Peace in
" ſo doing ; and altho' I have never been
" called to much Service, yet having one
" Talent committed to my Truſt, I have
" found an abſolute Neceſſity to improve
" the ſmall Portion of Grace received, and
" alſo to watch and guard againſt Tempta-
" tions, which I have had my Share of
" many Ways, but find none more danger-
" ous nor ſubtil than Self, the moſt cruel
" Foe, of which I am the more free to
" ſpeak in order to inform others, that they
" may beware and not attribute that Honour
" to Self which belongs to God : I have
" ſeen it in many Shapes, had many a
" Combat with it, and do rejoice in this,
" to ſee it under Foot and the Lord to be
" uppermoſt, there Self is of no Reputa-
" tion ; and that I may ſtill witneſs this,
" that as my Eye has been ſteadily fixed on
" my good Guide, who firſt found me out
" when alone in a deſart Land, and a Con-
" cern

" cern hath been raifed to follow him only
" in the Way of his Leadings, fo he alfo
" may have the Glory and Praife in the
" conducting me fafe thus far on my Jour-
" ney through many Difficulties and Straits,
" which but only to look back upon makes
" me fhudder at them, infomuch that ap-
" proaching Death appears a pleafant Re-
" leafe from a World of Trials and Befet-
" ments, which while here we are liable to ;
" and am ready to conclude my Work is
" almoft done, my Day near at an End,
" my Sun nigh fetting, in which the Curtain
" of the Night will be drawn over my earth-
" ly Tabernacle, which Pain and Weaknefs
" make to fhake, fo that I fuppofe what I
" do, I had need do quickly, for no Device
" or Work can there be done when the
" Spirit is departed ; wherefore having Love
" to my Fellow Citizens, as well as Good-
" will to Strangers, am willing for their
" Encouragement to leave this fmall Hint
" of the Goodnefs of God to a poor Worm,
" who am far from being able to fpeak one
" Half of what hath been done for me,
" only that Men may glorify God when
" they find my Footfteps, and confider that
" as weak as I have been, yet the great
" Condefcenfion of Divine Wifdom and
" Omnipotence is fuch, that now being
" confined as a Prifoner at Home by my
" incurable

" incurable Malady in the Flesh, my Spirit's
" at Liberty to praise God and give Glory
" to him, under a renewed Sense that I have
" so far fought the good Fight, and have
" been hitherto helped to keep the Faith,
" and I feel Peace to be my Reward, which
" makes ample Amends for all my Sorrows,
" yea, and present Pain, *Hallelujah to God*
" *on High, Peace on Earth, and Goodwill to*
" *Men,* saith my Soul : O let all cleave to
" him as to a most sure and certain Guide,
" who will not leave his comfortless, blessed
" be his Name ! but will come again and
" cause them to rejoice, and their Joy shall
" exceed the Joy of Harvest, when Corn
" and Wine increase.

" RACHEL CHANDLER.

" Esher, Ninth Month 1764."

DAVID COULSON, was born
at *Nottingham*, the 9th of the Fourth
Month 1713, of religious Parents, and educated in the Way of Truth ; in his Youth
was strongly addicted to vain Amusements
and Company, gratifying himself therein
for some Years ; his Father dying when he
was young, he was much labour'd with by

Q   his

his tender Mother, who with many Tears sought his Reformation, and which often affected him for a short Space ; but still his Inclination to Vanity was so great, that he stifled the Convictions of Truth.

About the twenty-first Year of his Age, happening to lodge in a damp Bed, an Inflamation in his Eyes followed, by which he lost his Sight, and being visited with Sickness was reduced very low ; nevertheless he did not break off from his Companions, their vain Conversation serving for an Excuse to divert him in his dull Situation, and altho' Pain and Sorrow of Heart were often his Portion, yet it was hard for him to take up the Cross and follow Christ in the Way of Self-denial, until about the twenty-sixth Year of his Age, when a powerful Visitation was extended, that he dared no longer to resist, and he had to see that if he did not join in therewith, it would be the last Visitation that would be afforded, he therefore consulted not with Flesh and Blood, but gave up to the Heavenly Vision ; of the Humiliation of which Day he would often speak with Reverence and Gratitude.

About the thirty-third Year of his Age, his Mouth was first opened to declare to others what God had done for his Soul, and
a Concern

a Concern was foon raifed in him to vifit the Churches, which notwithftanding his Want of Sight he gave up to, and excepting *Kent* and *Suffex*, he vifited all the Counties in *England*, and fome of them divers Times ; and thro' the merciful Care and Protection of his great Lord and Mafter, he was fo preferved as never to meet with any Fall or Accident to lay him up one Day in all his Travels.

For fome Years before his Death, he was afflicted with a fharp painful Diforder in his Stomach and Bowels, which rendred Travelling on Horfe-back impracticable, yet occafionally attended fome neighbouring or the Quarterly-meetings he belonged to ; under all which he had to remark, *That he had not neglected his Day's Work, in which,* he faid, *he found Peace, and that he could fay without Boafting, he never had omitted any thing that he apprehended his Duty.*

The next Day after his Return from the Circular-meeting at *Stourbridge* he was taken ill, and continued fo for fome Time, but at Times got out to Meetings. On the 24th of the Eleventh Month 1765, in the Afternoon he went to Meeting, and in the Evening had an acceptable Time in the Family, in which the Divine Life fpread like to the

Q 2   Odour

Odour of the precious Ointment to the
affecting many Minds.

In the Courſe of his Ilneſs, he dropt
many Heavenly Expreſſions, ſome of which
follow :

*O! it is a good Thing to live near the Lord
while in Health, for I find it now enough to
do to grapple with the Pain of the Body; but
I thank God I am quite eaſy whether I live or
die, Death is no Terror, for my Life is in
Chriſt, and the Lord ſweeteneth every bitter
Cup : But it is not ſo with thoſe who follow
lying Vanities, for they are forſaking their own
Mercies. The Lord can bring low and can
raiſe again at his Pleaſure. If I ſhould at
this Time be reſtored, I hope I ſhall be more
redeemed and brought nearer the Lord in that
pure Covenant of Life. I often think what
will become of them that are lukewarm in Religion, for if we keep ever ſo near the Lord,
and ſerve him with all our Mind and Strength,
we have nothing to ſpare, no, no; we are but
unprofitable Servants, we have done but that
which is our Duty. I pray God ſupport me
under all the Trials and Exerciſes of this
Day.*

To one who attended him, he ſaid to this
Effect : *Keep near the Lord and ſeek him with*
all

all thy Heart, for thou knows not how soon the Messenger may come, whether at Midnight, at Cockcrow, or at the Dawning of the Day. O let nothing hinder thee from seeking him! Look not at thy Poverty, for what signifies all the Greatness and Riches of this World, if we keep near the Lord he can be abundantly more than this unto us.

To another he said, *O poor Girl serve the Lord! Thou canst never do any thing better; the Lord loves an early Sacrifice, give him therefore the Sacrifice of thy Youth. I can say nothing more than to desire you to keep near the Lord, for I wish you all well; the Lord has been my Strength and Preserver, my all in all, the Lord is my Shepherd.*

To some Friends coming into the Room: *Now Friends, do you think it's fit to put off Repentance to such an Hour as this? O it is a sad Thing! for we all know we must die, it cannot be otherwise with any. But if we take not up our daily Cross and be regenerated and born again, we cannot see the Kingdom, much less enter into it. The Lord can bring low and raise again, blessed be his Holy Name, his Holy Will be done, come Life, come Death.*

The

The latter Part of the Day he fpoke little, but lay in a fweet Difpofition, defiring to be ftill, was fenfible to the laft, and quietly departed this Life, as one going into a fweet Sleep, about the fecond Hour in the Morning, the 9th of the Twelfth Month 1765. Aged fifty-two, a Minifter twenty Years.

LUCY ECROYD, Wife of *John Ecroyd*, of *Edge-End* in the County of *Lancafter*, and Daughter of *James* and *Ann Bradley*, of *Bromyard* in *Herefordfhire*, was mercifully vifited with the Manifeftation of Divine Grace while very young ; alfo the tender Care of an affectionaate Parent, who watched over her Children for Good, was bleffed to her in an eminent Manner : The wholfome Advice fhe was frequently concern'd to adminifter, made deep and awful Impreffions on her Mind, though fhe was foon deprived of this great Bleffing, her Mother dying when fhe was about thirteen Years of Age ; after which being expofed to unprofitable Company, fhe found the Truth of the Apoftle's Affertion, that *Evil Communications corrupt good Manners* ; for fhe was thereby drawn into Vanity, leaven'd into the Spirit of this World, and too much attach'd to its fading Enjoyments. In this

Time

Time of Forgetfulneſs and Departure from her firſt Love, ſhe met with many cloſe inward Trials and outward Diſappointments, finding no Reſt to her weary Soul, till paſſing thro' Judgment (by which Zion muſt be redeem'd) and enduring many ſore Conflicts, her Feet were mercifully turn'd into the Way of Peace.

About the nineteenth Year of her Age, her Mouth was firſt opened by Way of Teſtimony, being a good Example in Word, in Converſation, in Charity, in Faith and Purity, ſhe adorned the Doctrine of our Lord. Much might be added to commemorate her Worth, the Innocency of her Deportment and exemplary Conduct thro' the various Parts of her Service ; whether in her publick Station, or more private Service, let it ſuffice to ſay, her Heart was devoted to God, and from thence out of the good Treaſures thereof, ſhe brought forth Things new and old.

About the twenty-fourth Year of her Age ſhe viſited *London*, in Company with her beloved Friend *Rebecca Smith*, of *Nailſworth* in *Gloceſterſhire*, ſince deceaſed, where her Service was very acceptable, and indeed it may be recorded to the Memory of them both, they were inſtrumental of Good to many

many in their said Visit; and in all her Services being carefully concern'd to keep under the Guidance of the Holy Hand which put her forth, she was kept in the right Line, conducted therein with Safety through her Service, and was favour'd with the Return of Peace in her own Bosom.

In the latter Part of her Life when in Health, she frequently intimated a Persuasion that her Race was near over, expressing a fervent Desire, *That through Divine Mercy she might be enabled by patient Continuance in Well-doing, to hold out to the End.* Thus she retain'd her Integrity to the Close of Life, ever preferring Zion's Welfare before her chiefest Joy.

In her last Ilness she spoke but little, but her Patience under such great bodily Affliction, and the sweet Composure of her Countenance and Deportment, clearly evinced she had Access to the Place where Prayer is wont to be made.

She departed this Life the 26th of the First Month 1766, and was interred in Friends Burial-ground in *Marsden* in *Lancashire*. Aged forty-one Years.

JOSEPH

JOSEPH MILTHROP, a Member of *Pontefract* Monthly-meeting in *Yorkshire*, was educated in the Principles of the Church of *England* ; but as he advanced towards Man's Estate, being of a thoughtful Disposition, and unsatisfied with the Principles of his Education, he, after various Researches among the different Modes of Profession, join'd himself to the *Romish* Church, and for divers Years constantly attended their Worship, and strictly observed their ceremonial Institutions, for some Time firmly believing Christ Jesus to be the Author thereof ; tho' at Times he was led to believe there was a subduing of the Passions and a Renovation of Heart, which the truly Righteous experienced ; also a Fruition of inward Peace, which they at Times possessed : To all which he found himself, in great measure, a Stranger, which caused him many Times secretly to mourn and pour forth earnest Prayers to the Father of Mercies, that he might become a Partaker of the same happy Experience.

While he was thus exercised it came into his Mind to go to a Meeting of the People

R   called

called *Quakers*, for an Account of which take his own Words, in a Letter, *viz.*

" I sat at Ease a long Time, yet earnestly
" desired that if the Lord had any particular
" Regard to that People, or approved of
" their Manner of Worship, that he would
" make me sensible of it ; and being thus
" set and grown weary of silent Waiting,
" Divine Power seized upon my Body, Soul
" and Spirit, which caused me to break out
" into Abundance of Tears, and my Body
" greatly to tremble, then said I, *O Lord !*
" *why am I thus ?* To which inward Cry
" of mine, something which till then I
" knew not (tho' I had often felt a Measure
" of the same Power, tho' never to that
" Degree) answer'd, *If thou did but Love*
" *the Lord thy God with all thy Heart,*
" *Mind and Soul, that Love would be so*
" *prevalent over thee, that it would teach*
" *thee what to do, and what to eschew :* O
" the surprizing State I then found myself
" in ! How was my Heart then filled with
" Love, Peace and Joy unspeakable and
" full of Glory ! Soon after an honest
" Friend stood up in Tears and much
" Trembling, and said, *It is an excellent*
" *Thing if we can say of a Truth, Jesus*
" *Christ lives in us :* These Words reached
" my State, I then bowed in my Mind,
" adoring

" adoring the Divine Power that then
" influenced me, and said, *Dear Lord! if*
" *thou art he that I have long sought and*
" *mourn'd for, tell me, O thou that has*
" *ravished my Heart! what I should do to*
" *be saved, or to continue in thy Favour?*
" Upon which the humble Jesus, the Divine
" Bridegroom of my Soul, affectionately
" answer'd, *I require no Rite or ceremonial*
" *Worship of thee, but that thou give up thy*
" *Heart, it's there I would reign, it's there*
" *I would rule, and there I would be wor-*
" *ship'd in Spirit and Truth.*"

It was some Time before he could get
from under the Prejudices he had in Favour
of the *Roman* Church, but continued to
frequent both the Mass House and Friends
Meetings, until thro' a further Visitation by
an instrumental Means, he was effectually
reach'd, became a valuable and useful Member, exemplary in Conduct, careful to have
the Discipline maintain'd, and at Times was
concern'd in a short Testimony, which was
very acceptable; a peaceable Neighbour,
and being of extensive Knowledge, was
capable of advising in many Cases, which he
was always ready to do, demonstrating that
the living Divine Principle he had embraced,
led him to the Exercise of every *Christian*
Virtue.

For

For divers Years before his Death, he was at Times forely afflicted with the *Stone* and *Gravel*, the Acuteness of which he bore with exemplary Patience. His laft Ilnefs was fhort, and apparently attended with no Symptoms of Death till near the Time of his Departure, and though he was fuddenly called, yet not unprepared, for being afked a little before his Death, how he was, he expreffed himself thus : *I am pretty eafy, tho' not without fome bodily Pain, yet inward Comfort helps greatly* ; and added, *I am weary, weary, of this World, if it would pleafe Providence to take me to himfelf, O how acceptable it would be !*

He departed this Life the 3d, and was interred the 5th of the Seventh Month 1766, in Friends Burial-ground at *Burton*. Aged about fifty Years.

ALICE ALDERSON, Wife of *Ralph Alderfon*, of *Ravenftondale* in the County of *Weftmoreland*, was con-vinced of Truth in her young Years, and carefully abiding under its Divine Teachings confiftent to the Advice of the wife King *Solomon*, *Truft in the Lord with all thy Heart, and lean not to thy own Underftanding*, fhe came

came to receive a Gift in the Miniftry, and though for a confiderable Time in a few Words, yet greatly to the Edification of the Church, and being faithful in a little, witneffed an Increafe therein, and clothed with the Comlinefs of the Gofpel, fhe became valuable in the Lord's Houfe, devoting the Prime and Flower of her Youth, her Middle-age and Decline of Life, to his Service ; labouring diligently in the Caufe of Truth, both in this Nation, *Scotland* and *Ireland,* and once in *America* ; in all which her Labours of Love were well received, and tended much to the Edification of the Church. In her Miniftry, though fhe had not much human Learning, fhe was frequently furnifh'd with copious Expreffions well adapted to the Matter fhe had to deliver, deep and weighty in her Delivery, and enabled to fpeak feelingly to the State of Meetings and Individuals. She was remarkably diligent in attending Meetings when at Home, even to old Age, often fignifying that fhe believed none would be injured thereby in their outward Circumftances, as the Bleffings of Divine Providence upon the honeft Endeavours of the Faithful, would be an ample Recompence for all their Labour and feeming Lofs of Time. When old Age had fo far weaken'd her Conftitution that fhe could no longer attend Meetings, fhe retain'd the Divine

Anointing

Anointing which had been her Support thro', the various Stages of Life.

. The laſt Meeting ſhe was at, being the Day ſhe took to her Bed, ſhe had to revive the encouraging Invitation of the Prophet *Hoſea, Come and let us return unto the Lord; for he hath torn and he will heal us.; he hath ſmitten and he will bind us up ; after two Days will he revive us, in the third Day he will raiſe us up, and we ſhall live in his Sight : Then ſhall we know, if we follow on to know the Lord, his Going forth is prepared as the Morning, and he ſhall come unto us as the Rain, as the latter and former Rain unto the Earth.* Hoſea vi. 1, 2, 3.

' A few Days before her Departure, when ſome Friends were ſitting by her, ſhe was remarkably favour'd with the Overſhadowing of Divine Goodneſs, wherein ſhe had weightily to caution Miniſters and Elders to be exceeding watchful over their own Spirits, ſtrongly adviſing them to live in the Bond of Love and Unity, ſignifying ſhe clearly ſaw the ſubtil Enemy of Man's Happineſs endeavouring to draw them aſide, in order to mar or deface that Work which Divine Providence allotted them to be engaged in ; ſaying, *That the Lord had permitted her to be buffetted and brought low, even to the Gates*

of

of Hell, and had again in great Mercy lifted up her Head and given her the glorious Earneft of eternal Happinefs ; concluding in fervent Prayer for the fmall Meeting fhe was a Member of, and for all the fmall Gatherings of the Lord's People the World over.

In the Time of her Ilnefs fhe was afflicted with exceeding fharp Pain, which fhe bore with great Refignation, often praying. for Patience to bear what might be permitted to be laid on her. A Divine Serenity and Sweetnefs accompanied her laft Moments, that indeed it might be faid her Sun went down in Brightnefs.

She departed this Life on the 15th of the Eighth Month 1766, and was honourably interred in Friends Burial-ground the 18th of the fame at *Ravenftondale*, accompanied by many Friends and others. Aged eighty-eight, a Minifter fixty Years.

MARY

MARY WARING, late Wife of *Jeremiah Waring*, of *Wandsworth* in the County of *Surry*, and Widow of *Daniel Weston*, of *Ratcliffe*, was the Daughter of *Joseph Pace*, of *Southwark*, being favour'd with an early Visitation of Divine Love, she was clearly convinced of the evil Tendency of those undue Liberties whereby too many of our unwary Youth have been ensnared and gone astray ; and as she submitted to the sanctifying Operation of Truth, her Mind was redeem'd from a vain Conversation, and gradually fitted for the Work of the Ministry ; and being careful to improve the Gift received, she became an able Minister of the Gospel, found in Doctrine and skilful in dividing the Word aright.

She travelled much in the Service of Truth, having at sundry Times visited Friends in most of the Counties of *England* and *Wales*, and once most of the Colonies on the Continent of *America* ; in all which her Service was acceptable, and she labour'd much for the Preservation of good Order and Discipline in the Church. Of an open, generous and charitable Disposition, a Lover of Truth and

and the Friends of it, and was much beloved by them.

In her laſt Ilneſs, which was lingering and painful, being confined from Meeting about ſix Months, ſhe was favour'd with ſome acceptable Viſits from divers of her Friends, and would frequently ſay to them, *That her Mind was preſerved in a calm, peaceable Reſignation to the Divine Will.*

Among other Expreſſions of Weight which ſhe utter'd, the following are remembred, *viz. That ſhe believed herſelf near her End, for ſhe did not ſee that ſhe had any thing more of religious Duties to do* (meaning of a publick Nature) *for,* ſaid ſhe, *when I look at our own Meeting, I ſeem to have no Concern there ; and whereas I uſed to be anxious about the Quarterly-meetings, I now ſcarce think of them, yet,* added, *I wiſh well to the Cauſe, and believe it will proſper, but that a trying Day will come firſt.*

She departed this Life at *Wandſworth,* the 9th of the Tenth Month 1766, and was buried at *Ratcliffe* near *London* the 16th of the ſame, attended by many Friends. Aged fifty-four, a Miniſter thirty Years.

S CANDIA

CANDIA CORBYN, Wife of *John Corbyn*, of the City of *Worcester*, was born about the Year 1671, at *Pontypool* in *Monmouthshire*, and about the eighteenth Year of her Age, was reached by Truth through the powerful Miniſtry of *Thomas Wilson*, which taking deep Root in her Heart ſhe brought forth good Fruits.

In a few Years ſhe received a Gift in the Miniſtry, in the Exerciſe of which ſhe was found and clear, and evidently favoured with the Renewings of that Divine Life which preſerved her freſh and green; being often tenderly concern'd both in Teſtimony and Supplication on Behalf of the Youth, that their tender Minds might be preſerved from the many Snares that lie in the Way, and be ſo formed and enlarged by the Divine Hand, as to become living Branches in the true Vine and ſerviceable Members in Society.

She was frequently engaged to bear Teſti-mony to the Univerſality and Sufficiency of the Grace of God, extended through the *Chriſtian* Diſpenſation, to all Mankind; and ſhe earneſtly labour'd that Friends would retain

retain a grateful Senfe of the Liberties we now enjoy, to hold our religious Meetings without Moleftation ; often recounting the many Hardfhips, which fhe well remembred, our ancient Friends were permitted to undergo for the Trial of their Faith.

She continued a diligent Attender of Meetings both for Worfhip and Difcipline, in Love and Charity as a Mother in *Ifrael,* faithfully difcharging her Duty towards all, hofpitable to Strangers, a Friend to all, efpecially the Poor, Fatherlefs and Widow ; in her Connections in Life, a fteady Pattern of Piety and Virtue, fo that it may be faid, in Doctrine and Practice, the Dew of Heaven refted on her Branches even to very advanced Age.

Her laft Ilnefs being but fhort, fhe calmly departed this Life the 28th of the Fourth Month 1767, and her Remains were decently interred in Friends Burial-ground at *Worcefter* the 3d of the Fifth Month following: Aged ninety-fix, a Minifter feventy-three Years.

Although no Expreffions of this ancient Friend are preferved, yet as through a long Courfe of Years fhe was preferved unfpotted and ftrong in her Love, as was the Cafe of

Caleb

Caleb formerly, the Account is worthy of
Prefervation, that all may fee and be encouraged, that if they keep to this living Divine
Principle, they will be enabled to hold out
to the End.

RICHARD HIPSLEY, a
Member of *Claverbam* Monthly-meeting in the County of *Somerfet*, was born in
the Parifh of *Church-hill* in the faid County
about the Year 1708, his Parents were
religious faithful Friends, who carefully
educated him in the Way of Truth, and as
he grew in Years he grew in Grace, by
which his Underftanding was opened and
enlarged, that about the thirty fifth Year of
his Age his Mouth was firft opened in a
publick Teftimony, in which he was very
diffident and cautious. And the Lord who
knew his Sincerity was pleafed fo to enlarge
his Heart therein, that he became an able
Minifter, and being fitted and prepared he
could no longer withhold, but was concern'd
to vifit divers Parts of this Nation and
Ireland, to general Satisfaction.

He was eminently qualified to fpeak a
Word in Seafon, in Monthly and Quarterly-
meetings, which he was diligent in attending,

as

as well as frequently the Yearly-meeting in *London*.

He was a Man of a chearful Spirit, pleasant and affable in Converfation, a good Hufband and tender Father, a kind Neighbour, doing to all as he would be done unto ; his Houfe and Heart were open to entertain his Friends.

He was afflicted with a long Ilnefs, the *Dropfy*, and was often in great Pain, which he bore with much Patience, believing his Departure drew near, frequently expreffing his Refignation to the Divine Will, and often fignified to them who vifited him in his Ilnefs, *That it appeared to him that all was well, and that he had nothing to do but to die.*

He quietly departed this Life the 8th of the Fifth Month 1767, and was buried in Friends Burial-ground at *Sedcott* the 13th of the fame, accompanied by a large Number of Friends and others, where feveral living and powerful Teftimonies were borne, to the Satisfaction and Comfort of thofe who were prefent.

EDMUND

EDMUND PECKOVER, of *Wells* in *Norfolk*, was the Son of *Joseph* and *Catharine Peckover*, both Perfons of great Efteem in the Society. He was early favour'd with a divine Vifitation, of which a more particular Account cannot be given than is in a Paper found in his own Handwriting.

"The tender Dealings," fays he, " of
" the Almighty, with me in my Youth,
" being often frefh in my Remembrance,
" brings a moft greatful Senfe thereof over
" my Mind, under which I cannot but with
" Reverence commemorate the fame. It
" was no fmall Advantage to me, that I
" was favour'd with religious and godly
" Parents, whofe Concern and Care to bring
" me and the reft of their Children up in
" the Nurture and Admonition of the Lord
" was great: And what I look upon as very
" remarkable, is, that before I arrived at
" an Age capable to retain thofe good and
" wholfom Admonitions, which in the Wif-
" dom of God, they often communicated to
" me, I felt the good Hand of the Lord
" at Work in me, in a Manner fuitable to
" my tender Capacity, impreffing upon my
" Heart

" Heart a living Senſe of his Greatneſs and
" Goodneſs, which often brought me under
" much Awfulneſs and Fear, dreading to
" do any thing that I knew was not well-
" pleaſing in his Sight : Herein I could
" diſtinguiſh that I had Peace and Satis-
" faction, and met with Encouragement in
" myſelf, beyond what I am able to expreſs ;
" and when I had been drawn away into
" any thing which tended to hinder my
" Growth in that which I found to my Soul's
" Advantage, Sorrow and Trouble took
" hold of me, under a Senſe whereof, I
" often made Vows and Promiſes, that I
" would never join with the like again,
" which being my firſt Fruits before the
" Lord, I believe he had a tender Regard
" to, and often aſſiſted me to perform thoſe
" Covenants, which thro' ſome good Mea-
" ſure of Divine Influence I then entered
" into.

" In the Time of this Exerciſe, great and
" many were the Conflicts I had to encounter
" with ; but, to the Praiſe of his great
" Name, I ſpeak it, his compaſſionate
" fatherly Care was over me, and always
" attended me with ſuch a Portion of his
" Divine and ſaving Grace, that I knew
" Preſervation thereby thro' Things of the
" moſt trying and pinching Nature, in the
" Experience

" Experience whereof Thankfulnefs would
" arife."

Thus through Faithfulnefs to the Divine
Manifeftations, he was early anointed to
preach the Gofpel, even in his Minority,
while at the School of our Friend *Gilbert
Thompfon* (mention'd in the fore Part of
this Treatife) in the fifteenth Year of his
Age: And as he abode in Faithfulnefs he
increafed in his Gift, and in the Year 1714,
and in the eighteenth Year of his Age, in
Company with *Edward Upfher* of *Colchefter*,
he vifited divers Counties, and alfo *Ireland*
about the twentieth Year of his Age, in
Company with *George Gibfon*, as well as
moft Parts of this Nation, *Scotland*, *Ireland*
and *America*, in the fucceeding Part of his
Time.

He was indeed an Elder worthy of double
Honour, being of an exemplary Life and
unftain'd Character, and in the Exercife of
his Gift frequently opened and enlarged in
Divine Counfel, and as a Cloud filled with
Cœleftial Rain to the reviving and Refrefhment of the living Heritage of God;
zealous for the Profperity of the Church and
for the Ingathering of all, he fpared not to
fpend himfelf in the Strength of his Days,
and Divine Goodnefs was pleafed to preferve

him

him a ſtrong Man and an able Miniſter for a long Courſe of Years. He uſually deliver'd himſelf with great Fervency in the flowing forth of Divine Love upon his Spirit.

About three Years before his Deceaſe, he received a Shock of a *Paralytic* Kind, which both in his own Apprehenſion and that of his Friends, ſeem'd to threaten him with a haſty Diſſolution ; under this affecting Viſitation, by the Account of a Relation who viſited him the ſame Evening, he was graciouſly preſerved in a broken, tender, living Frame, and expreſſed himſelf after this Manner : *That he had now the Satisfaction of a good Conſcience, and of having diſcharged himſelf in the Duty required of him; according to the Ability afforded him* ; declaring at the ſame Time, *the great Conſolation he inwardly enjoyed.* The next Morning after a ſhort Sleep, and taking ſome little Refreſhment, he was ſomewhat revived, and ſignified, *He was well pleaſed that his outward Affairs were ſettled, and was fully ſatisfied with the Manner in which they were ordered ; that he was entirely reſigned to the Diſpoſal of all-wiſe Providence, whether it might be to lengthen his Days or to take him hence ; but he felt a bleſſed Aſſurance, and found the Lord who had been his Support thro' many Trials, from his Youth to his advanced Years, ſtill to be near*

T   *him*

him, and could experimentally say, his Redeemer lived, who hath ever been the Strength of his faithful People, and who had brought to pass many Things in his no short Pilgrimage, which to outward Appearance seem'd very unlikely.

After this he lay in a sweet and quiet Frame, and his Pain lessening, he appeared pretty chearful, and in Time he became so far restored as to be able to go Abroad in a Carriage, but with considerable Difficulty to himself. And tho' in common Conversation his Apprehension and Memory seem'd much impaired, yet his publick Appearance in Meetings continued sound, consistent and savoury.

A few Months before his Death, he was rendred totally unable to attend Meetings, and continued gradually to decline, and the gracious Lord, who had been his Strength and Stay in the Prime of his Life, supported him in his last Moments, for then he appear'd to be favour'd with a comfortable Foretaste of that glorious Immortality which is prepared for the Righteous; for tho' he was deprived of bodily Strength to speak so distinctly as usual, yet he was sufficiently understood to intimate the inexpressible Joy and Felicity that he felt, and seem'd to pass

away

away as with an Heavenly Song of Divine Praife in his Mouth.

He departed this Life at *Wells*, the 19th of the Seventh Month 1767, and his Remains were interred at *Fakenham* the 22d; after a large and folemn Meeting of Relations, Friends and Neighbours. Aged about feventy-two, a Minifter about fifty-feven Years.

ELIZABETH ROBERTS, late Wife of *William Roberts*, of *Edmundfbury* in *Suffolk*, was Daughter of *James Morley*, of *Wymondbam* in *Norfolk*. This our Friend was early impreffed with a Senfe of Religion, which attending to, fhe grew in Grace and in the Knowledge of the Truth, and about the twenty-fecond Year of her Age was raifed up to bear Teftimony thereto, in which fhe faithfully laboured in much Zeal and *Chriftian* Love for fome Years. In Conduct and Behaviour fhe was exemplary, as well as in Word and Doctrine inftructive, devoting the Prime of her Youth and Health to the Service of Truth.

About two Years before her Deceafe fhe fell into a great Decline of bodily Strength,

which

which difabled her from Travelling ; but
fhe retain'd a lively Senfe of the Divine
Goodnefs, rejoicing, *That fhe had in the Time
of Health and Strength been diligent to do her
Duty according to Ability received.*

She bore her Affliction which was great,
with becoming Patience and Refignation,
and the Day fhe died, *prayed the Lord to be
with her to the laft and give her an eafy
Paffage,* which it's believed fhe happily experienced, paffing away without any apparent
Uneafinefs, at the Age of forty-one Years,
the 9th of the Tenth Month 1767.

K EZIA DAY, late Wife of
Samuel Day, of *Stanfted Mountfitchet*
in the County of *Effex,* was vifited in her
tender Years, and being faithful, had, at
Times, to recommend her Friends to the
internal Teacher, and being careful not to
move in the Wind, Earthquake or Fire,
but waiting to hear the ftill fmall Voice,
her Appearances were truly fatisfactory and
comfortable to the Living.

In the Courfe of her bodily Weaknefs
fhe was enabled to bear her Affliction with
Patience, and being wean'd from a Dependance

ance on Visibles, her Attention seem'd to be fixed on an everlasting Inheritance. She was favour'd with much Serenity, and a comfortable Evidence, *That he who had been her Support in Life, would preserve her to a happy Conclusion in his Favour, and that she should enter the Joy of her Lord ;* her lively Exhortations and sincere Breathings to God near her End were to the Comfort and Edification of those present, to whom she had to declare, *That the Truth had been her Preservation until that Time ;* having to acknowledge the Riches of Divine Love. She desired, *That those with whom she was most nearly connected would give her up freely, and not grieve too much, but rather rejoice in Hope :* At another Time, she said, *She hoped she had been faithful to what had been required.*

She quietly departed this Life without Sigh or Groan, on the 20th of the Second Month 1768, and was interred in Friends Burial-ground at *Stansted* aforesaid, the 28th of the same. Aged about twenty-eight Years, and a Minister about six Years.

BENJAMIN

BENJAMIN TROTTER, of the City of *Philadelphia*, was born in that City about the Year 1699, and was one whom the Lord early vifited and reached to by the Reproof of his Divine Light and Grace, for thofe youthful Vanities and corrupt Converfation which by Nature he was prone to and purfued (to the Grief of his pious Mother who was religioufly concern'd to reftrain him.) But as he became obedient to the renewed Vifitations of the Heavenly Call, denying himfelf of thofe Things he was reproved for, he not only ceafed from doing Evil, but learned to do well; and continuing faithful, became an Example of Plainnefs and Self-denial, for which he fuffered much Scoffing and Mocking of thofe who had been his Companions in Folly; yet he neither fainted nor was turn'd afide by the Reproaches of the Ungodly, which thus fell to his Lot for his plain Teftimony againft their evil Conduct.

In the twenty-fixth Year of his Age, he appeared in the Work of the Miniftry, and labour'd therein in much Plainnefs and godly Sincerity, adorning the Doctrine he preach'd by a humble circumfpect Life and Converfation,

sation, being exemplary in his Diligence and
Industry to labour honestly for a Livelihood,
though often in much bodily Infirmity and
Weakness, desiring as he sometimes expressed,
*That he might owe no Man any thing but
Love.* His inoffensive Openness and Affa-
bility, drawing many of different Denominations to converse with him, he had some
seasonable Opportunities of admonishing and
rebuking the evil Doer and evil Speaker,
which he did in the Plainness of an upright
Zeal for the Promotion of Piety and Virtue,
tempered with true Brotherly-kindness and
Charity, respecting not the Person of the
Proud, nor of the Rich because of his Riches,
but with *Christian* Freedom declaring the
Truth to his Neighbour, and was thus in
private as well as publick, a Preacher of
Righteousness.

He at several Times visited most of the
Meetings in the Provinces of *Pennsylvania*
and *New-Jersey*, and some in the adjacent
Provinces; and for upwards of forty Years
was a diligent Attender of our religious
Meetings in the City of *Philadelphia*, and
zealously concern'd for the Maintenance of
our *Christian* Discipline in Meekness and true
Charity; careful in the Exercise of that Part
of pure Religion, visiting the Widow and
Fatherless in their Afflictions, and often
qualified

qualified to adminiſter Relief and Conſolation to their dejected Minds.

In his publick Teſtimony, a little before his laſt Sickneſs, he expreſſed his Apprehenſions, *That his Time would be ſhort*, and fervently exhorted *to Watchfulneſs and Care, to keep our Lamps trimmed and our Lights burning*, and urged *the Neceſſity of being prepared to meet the Bridegroom, as not knowing at what Hour he would come.*

In his laſt Sickneſs, which laſted upwards of ſix Weeks, he underwent great Difficulty and Pain, being afflicted with the *Aſthma* and *Dropſy*, which he bore with exemplary Patience and Reſignation, and was never heard to utter a Murmur or Complaint, but frequently expreſſed his Thankfulneſs that he had not more Pain ; and was often engaged in Prayer, *That he might be preſerved in Patience to the End*, which was graciouſly granted him, ſo that he was capable of ſpeaking to the Comfort and Edification of thoſe who viſited him.

He departed this Life in the Third Month 1768, and after a ſolemn Meeting, in which ſeveral living Teſtimonies were borne, was interred in Friends Burial-ground in that
City,

City, the 24th of the fame. Aged upwards of fixty-eight Years.

REBECCA SMITH, late of *Nailfworth* in the County of *Gloucefter*, was one who was a good Example in Purity of Life and Manners, fincerely loved the Truth, and diligently fought the Promotion thereof. Through the Operation of Divine Love on her Mind in her young Years, fhe preferred the Caufe of Truth, and about the twenty-ninth Year of her Age received a Call to the Miniftry, and being inwardly fenfible that a Difpenfation of the Gofpel was committed to her, fhe delayed not with vain Confultations, but readily fubmitted to that proving Engagement, and chearfully furrendring her Will to Divine Requirings, foon grew fkilful in dividing the Word; thereby evidently fhewing to ferious awaken'd Minds, that in this as in other religious Services, the Lord loveth a chearful Giver.

She was a diligent, exact Attender of Meetings, and there was fomething fecretly inftructive in that weighty, retired Manner in which fhe ufually fat in them, often long in Silence, being careful to feel Divine Life precede and put forth to Service, and when

U   raifed

raifed in Miniftry, not to exceed the Opening
of the Gift : Thus her Teftimony was preferved clear and edifying, truly acceptable to
Friends, both at Home and Abroad where
fhe travelled, being alfo ferviceable in the
Difcipline.

Having known many deep inward Afflictions and clofe Refinings, fhe obtained
the Tongue of the Learned, and often had
a Word to fpeak in due Seafon. Thus
ferving her Generation, fhe fulfilled the Miniftry fhe received to teftify to the Sufficiency
of Divine Grace, and finifhed her Courfe
with Joy the 28th of the Eleventh Month
1768. Aged fifty-four Years.

THOMAS DANN, a Member
of *Dorking* Monthly-meeting, in the
County of *Surry*, was born at *Nutfield* in
the faid County, of honeft and religious
Parents. In his young Years he was much
addicted to Vanity, yet by the tender Vifitations of kind Providence he was preferved
from grofs Evils ; and as he grew to Man's
Eftate, thro' the fame gracious Vifitations,
the Beauty and Comlinefs of this World was
ftain'd in his View, and he fitted for Service,
into which he was called about the thirtieth

Year

Year of his Age. He was a Preacher of Righteoufnefs, not only in Word and Doctrine, but in Life and Converfation ; a diligent Attender of Meetings for Worfhip and Difcipline, earneftly recommending Friends to an humble Waiting on the Lord, for Counfel and Direction in the Management of the Affairs of the Church ; and tho' not concern'd to travel much Abroad, yet he vifited fome adjacent Counties to good Satisfaction. A juft Reprover of the Libertine, but very tender to the Sincere-hearted, ready to give Advice and Counfel to thofe who ftood in need, much concern'd for Peace, and often inftrumental in compofing Differences amongft his Friends and Neighbours ; a Sympathizer with the Afflicted, liberal and compaffionate to the Poor, a loving Hufband and tender Father, yet not indulging his Children in any thing he believed inconfiftent with the Truth, a good Mafter and a fincere Friend.

It pleafed the Lord fome Time before his Departure, to give him a Senfe that his Day was near at an End, his Work almoft done, and that all was well with him ; and he often expreffed in his Ilnefs, *He found nothing ftand in his Way* ; in the fore Part of which his Pain was very great, but he was fervently engaged to befeech the Lord to grant him

Patience,

Patience, that he might endure it with becoming Refignation, which was mercifully afforded him ; for which, and the many repeated Favours received, he had to praife and magnify God's Holy Name, and to declare with *Jacob* of old, *That the Lord had been with him all his Life long* ; in which comfortable Affurance he quietly departed this Life, the 23d of the Second Month, and his Corps accompanied by many Friends and Neighbours, was decently interred at *Rygate*, the 1ft of the Third Month 1769. Aged fixty-five, a Minifter thirty-five Years.

JOHN BURTON, a Member of *Sedbergh* Monthly-meeting in *Yorkfhire*, was born at *Dent* within the Compafs of that Meeting, and was favoured with the Vifitation of Divine Love in his young Years, whereby he came to fee the Emptinefs of all mere outward Profeffion and Performances, and that no Worfhip would find Acceptance with his Creator but that performed in Spirit and Truth ; under the Influences thereof he was brought into Communion with our Society, and by taking heed to the inward Anointing, and abiding faithful thereto, agreeable to 1 *John* ii. 27. he arrived to a good Degree of *Chriftian*

Experience,

Experience, and to fee the Neceffity of Regeneration, the refining Hand working powerfully in him, in order to fit him for further Service, unto which he was called in the early Part of his Time, and became truly devoted to the great Mafter's Ufe, to be led and conducted according to his Requirings.

Tho' he had but little human Learning, he was often led forth in a living powerful Teftimony, in Matter exceeding copious and pertinent, enabled to divide the Word aright, and to fpeak feelingly to the States of the People, being indued with a large Gift in the Miniftry, often dipped into great Sufferings with the Seed of Life that lay oppreffed in the Hearts of many ; but when he who was his Life did appear, he was as a Holy Flame to the warming and comforting the Hearts of the Afflicted, and as a fharp Sword to the Lukewarm and Carelefs, tender and affectionate to thofe who were young in the Miniftry, greatly rejoicing when the Word of Life arofe in them, tho' declared but in a few Expreffions, treating them with much Love and Refpect, left they fhould fink under Difcouragement.

In the Courfe of his *Chriftian* Progrefs he had to vifit *Ireland*, and divers of the
Northern

Northern Counties, and *London* several
Times : He also visited the *American* Colonies ; in all which he was conducted much
to the Satisfaction of Friends. Tho' of a
free, chearful Disposition and Behaviour,
yet was he properly guarded, being a plain
Man, bearing a faithful Testimony against
the Pride and vain Shew of the present Age.
He was a Man that was truly engaged for
the good Order of the Church, and that the
Line of Discipline might be kept to, waiting in those Meetings in an humble Manner
for Divine Direction, whereby he was qualified in much Love to speak with Authority
and Judgment, being clear sighted in difficult Matters.

In the latter Part of his Time, he was
much confined at Home through bodily Infirmities ; when visited by Friends he received them in much Love, his Mind still re-
taining strong and hearty Desires that the
Church of Christ might flourish and appear
in her ancient Beauty, and Zion keep her
Garments unspotted of the World.

In the Beginning of his Ilness, he in a
very moving pathetic Manner, bewailed
to some Friends who visited him, the Loss
the Church sustained by many pursuing the
Riches

Riches and Grandeur of this perishing World, instead of durable Riches and Righteousness.

About two Days before he died, he expressed himself to some intimate Friends who visited him, *That he had passed through many deep and humbling Baptisms in the Course of his own Experience, and on the Account of the Backsliding of many under our Name, and some of his own Family; but now they seemed to him to be all over, being filled with Light, Divine Consolation and Peace on every hand, which was enough for all; and that it would be the happy Experience of all such who served the Lord in Sincerity, and had Zion's Welfare at Heart: But that a fearful and terrible Day would overtake the Careless, if there was not a turning to the Lord while the Offers of Mercy were extended.*

He likewise said, *That when he believed it his Duty to leave his Family and the near Connections of Life, he had never omitted one Journey on Truth's Account, which he had then great Peace in.*

Thus this Servant of the Lord departed in Faith and full Assurance of a Resting-place with the Righteous, the 23d of the Third Month 1769, in the eighty-seventh

Year

Year of his Age, having been a Minister about sixty Years, and was interred in Friends Burial-ground in *Dent*, a large and solemn Meeting being held on the Occasion.

WILLIAM RECKITT, of *Wainfleet* in *Lincolnshire*, having, through a variety of Exercises and many trying Seasons, given evident Marks of Stability of Mind, and through a firm Confidence in that Hand which led him forth into Service, hath filled up his Duty; for the Encouragement of others that they also may follow the Footsteps of those that are gone, altho' under the most trying Seasons, the following Account of him claims a Place in these Memoirs.

He was born in the Year 1706 and educated among Friends, and about the thirty-sixth Year of his Age came forth in the Work of the Ministry, in much Simplicity and Innocency, to the Satisfaction of Friends, it being in the Life of Truth, the only Authority of all true Ministry, in which he laboured faithfully in divers Parts of this Nation and *Ireland*; and about the Year 1756 a Concern came on him to visit *America*, and with his Friends Unity and Concurrence

currence he embarked for *Philadelphia*, but was soon after they fail'd, taken by a Privateer and carried into *Morlaix*, and he through the Favour of a *French* Merchant there, who voluntarily became his Security, was sent to *Carhaix* in *Brittany*, where he resided five Months before his Liberty was obtained ; during which he was preserved in Meekness and Innocence ; and by Accounts from thence, his Lamb-like Nature gain'd much on some of the *French* Inhabitants, and led them to treat him with much Respect, and he had several Opportunities with them to his Satisfaction, particularly with the chief Magistrate of the Town. In a Letter to a Friend he gives this Account of it :

" He asked me many Questions concern-
" ing our Principles, which I answered
" short, but so full that he made no Ob-
" jections, and I was thankful in my Mind
" it was so, for it was somewhat difficult
" for the young Man my Interpreter, tho'
" he is always ready to assist me when I
" have Occasion. When I got home to
" my solitary Dwelling, and considered how
" often the Lord had appeared on my Be-
" half, and had been my Advocate, I was
" much bowed in Thankfulness before him.
" I much desire I may be remembred by
" you" meaning Friends, " for Good, when

X   " it

" it is well with you, for I am afraid I
" fhould not hold out to the End, or that
" I fhould bring fome Difhonour to Truth :
" O how grievous a Thing I have thought
" it would be if I fhould now bring up an
" evil Report of the good Land, and fo
" thereby difcourage poor Souls that have
" fet their Faces thither-ward ! I had rather,
" if it was confiftent with the Will of my
" Heavenly Father, be gathered Home in
" a good Time : My Fears have all been
" concerning myfelf, for furely I never faw
" more of my own Weaknefs, it hath been
" indeed a fearching Time to me ; and
" yet it fprings in my Heart to fay, If the
" Lord hath any Delight in me, he will
" bring me fafe through all : He knows the
" Integrity of my Heart, I did not fet out
" in a forward Spirit, but in his Counfel,
" and in it at this Time I ftand ; he knows
" beft what will be moft for his own Ho-
" nour. And as to what will become of
" this earthen Tabernacle, it feems to be
" the leaft of my Care, fo that I may finifh
" my Courfe with Joy."

After his Return from *France* he returned
Home, but the Concern remaining, in about
four Weeks he came back to *London*, and
again embarked, and arrived fafe at *Phila-*
delphia in the Year 1757, and after vifiting

moft

most of the Provinces on that Continent, to the Comfort and Edification of Friends, he embarked for *Barbadoes*, but was again taken and carried into *Martinico*, and after about two Weeks Confinement, through the Favour of the Commiffary, he embarked on board a Cartel Ship for the Ifland called St. *Kitts*, where he had feveral Meetings, and alfo at *Nevis*, where he had two Meetings ; at one of which a Prieft ftood up, and addreffing the People, told them, *The everlafting Gofpel had been preached among them that Day* ; and recommended it to the Obfervation and Practice of all prefent : And our Friend declared, *He never felt the Power of Truth rife fo high as at thofe Meetings.* After which, finding his Mind clear, altho' invited to ftay and have more Meetings, and was told, *Many of the Inhabitants were Defcendants from Friends*, he returned to St. *Kitts*, fo called, and foon after embarked for *Philadelphia*, and from thence for *London*. In about three Years after, he again vifited *America*, and divers Parts of this Nation.

In private Life, an affectionate Hufband and tender Father, and kind Friend, adorning the Gofpel with a becoming Converfation : Thus perfevering on in a Courfe of Virtue, about a Year before his Deceafe, he wrote again to the Friend before mentioned in the

X 2   following

following Manner, which shews the Integrity of his Heart continued :

" The Sap of Life lies very deep in the
" Root, and that must be waited for in those
" sorrowful and pinching Times I have met
" with, and yet I have had a comfortable
" Hope raised in me of late that all would
" be well in the End, the Prospect of which
" to me hath seemed exceeding pleasant,
" and if safe should much desire it might be
" hastened ; but that's not my proper Busi-
" ness to look for, or desire the Reward
" before the Day's Work is finished. I
" have served a good Master, but have
" ever looked on myself one of the weakest
" of his Servants ; yet have endeavour'd to
" come up in faithful Obedience to his Will
" made manifest in me, and in this now I
" have great Peace, and an Assurance of an
" Inheritance that will never fade away, if
" I continue in the Way of well-doing to
" the End of the Race."

After which he visited the City of *London*, which he often hinted he thought it might be the last Time ; but his Love and Integrity to the Cause of Truth continued, and it was evident the Fervency of his Mind was as strong as ever.

His

His Ilnefs was very fhort, he was taken with a Fit of the *Ague* at Night, and next Morning about Four departed this Life, the 6th of the Fourth Month 1769, and was interred in Friends Burial-ground the 9th of the fame. Aged about fixty-three Years.

JOSHUA TOFT, an ancient Friend of *Leek* in *Staffordfhire*, was favour'd in the early Part of his Life with the Knowledge of the blefled Truth, and by Obedience thereto became when young in Years an Example of Religion and Virtue.

His Concerns in Bufinefs at that Time requiring his being much from Home, and to be converfant with thofe unacquainted with the circumfpeck Conduct and Manner of Behaviour of the People he had join'd in Communion, he was expofed in the youthful Part of his Life to fevere and ill Treatment; but his Mind being clothed with the Patience of the Holy Word, he experienced by its blefled Fruits of Meeknefs and Love, the Ignorance of foolifh Men not only filenced, but fometimes their Wrath and Enmity, through his faithful Teftimony, turn'd into Refpect and Friendfhip; and though his Beginning in the World was fmall, yet being
blefled

bleffed by Providence, whofe is the Earth and the Fulnefs thereof, as well as the Dew of Heaven, he was fatisfied with a moderate Competency, and in the full Strength of Life and Flow of Bufinefs, which would have enabled him to accumulate much Wealth, with noble Fortitude, believing it to be required of him, he declined Trade, more fully to devote himfelf to his great Lord and Mafter's Service in the Gofpel-Miniftry, into which he had been called about the thirty-fecond Year of his Age, in which he diligently and faithfully laboured many Years in various Parts of this Nation and *Ireland*, to the Comfort and Edification of the Church and his own Peace.

Near twenty Years before his Deceafe he was difabled from travelling much from Home, being feized with a Diforder in his Head, which affected at Times his Underftanding, and deprived him for more than fourteen Years of the latter Part of his Life of Sight ; after the Lofs of which, his Faculties became as ftrong as before, and his Underftanding perfect, which continued to the laft. With exemplary Patience, Chearfulnefs and Refignation, he bore great Affliction of Body, as well as Deprivation of Sight, fignifying, *All that was laid upon him*
                                                    was

*was in Love and intended for his Good, and
hoped he should receive it as such.*

A Day or two before his Departure, he
said, *He had been much confolated, having
received a moft gracious Promife, I have been
with thee, I am with thee, and will be with
thee.*

He quietly departed this Life the 15th of
the Eighth Month 1769, aged upwards of
eighty, a Minifter forty-eight Years, and
was interred in Friends Burial-ground at *Leek*,
on which Occafion the fame ever glorious
Truth that had been with him in the Beginning and Clofe of his Pilgrimage thro' Life,
was manifefted to the renewed Encouragement of many, to prove for themfelves
likewife, that the Gifts and Callings of God
are without Repentance.

R ICHARD REYNOLDS,
late of *Winterburn* in *Gloucefterfhire*,
was born at *Banbury* in the County of *Oxford*,
and in his very early Years manifefted a
religious Difpofition, and knew in fome Degree the purifying Hand of Divine Goodnefs
to fit him for Service, fo that about the
twentieth

twentieth Year of his Age he appeared in the Ministry to the Satisfaction of Friends.

He resided for many Years in the City of *Bristol*, where his Business before he retreated from it to *Winterburn* lay, which he was induced to do from a Desire of withdrawing from the incumbring Pursuit of temporal Things, often expressing the Hurt sustained by an over Solicitude for Things of this Life.

A considerable Time before his Decease, he was taken with a sudden Indisposition of Body as he was travelling on the Account of temporal Concerns, and his Mind became alarmed with this Instruction, *Set thy House in Order* ; to which he diligently attended, in a spiritual Sense especially.

In the Course of his Ilness he appear'd much resigned to Divine Disposal, and utter'd many instructive Sayings to those who were with him very intelligibly and with clear Understanding, expressing, *That the Father's Love is the best Cordial. This is a trying Time. We had need to lay up a good Foundation against the Time to come. That the peaceful State of his Mind was all owing to Divine Goodness, for to us, O Lord! belongeth Shame and Confusion of Face.* He was under deep
Travail

Travail of Spirit, *That he might be thoroughly
purified and made meet for the Kingdom* ; and
was enabled to pray, *That the Lord would
lift up the Light of his Countenance, and thro'
Christ forgive all his Omissions*, which there
is good Reason to believe was granted. With
much Sensibility he mentioned the Saying of
the *Leper* to Christ, *Lord! if thou wilt thou
canst make me clean* ; and the gracious Answer, *I will, be thou clean*. That which lay
with the greatest Weight and Dissatisfaction
on his Mind was, *His having been too closely
attached to worldly Things*. And a little
before his Departure, he said in an affecting
Manner, *Too much Assiduity! Too much Care!
I might have been a better Example! So much
Care and Pains alienate the Mind : The Lord
is merciful, I hope he will forgive me that
Sin. I would have you take Warning by me.*
This last Saying he repeated with much
Concern, and then laying in a composed
Manner for a few Hours, quietly expired at
Bath, the 8th of the Twelfth Month 1769,
and was buried in Friends Burial-ground near
the *Friars* in *Bristol* the 15th. Aged about
sixty Years, a Minister about forty Years.

Y   JAMES

JAMES WILSON, of *Kendall*, was born in the Parish of *Kirby-Lonsdale* in *Westmoreland* in the Year 1677 ; his Parents *Edmund* and *Jane Wilson*, educated him in the Way of the Church of *England*. When young in Years his Heart was much bent to seek after real Religion, being uneasy with the dead Formalities in which he was educated, his Soul thirsting after the Enjoyment of the Lord's Presence ; he in this Time of seeking after Good, devoted much of his leisure Time to reading the Holy Scriptures, especially the New Testament ; in the Perusal whereof his Mind was more informed, tendred and broken, than by all the instrumental Labour he had partook of. Some Time after being convinced of the Principles of Truth, he joined our Society ; and in the thirtieth Year of his Age he came forth in the Work of the Ministry, and was soon drawn into, and eminently qualified for much extensive Labour in the Church, and amongst the People in *Great-Britain* and *Ireland* : He devoted much of the Prime and Strength of his Life to the Service of Truth, diligently labouring in the Ability it gives both at Home and Abroad, to the Honour of the great Name and the Edification

tion of many; frequently attending Meetings on publick Occasions, and divers appointed in fresh Places, wherein his Labours were well received, and he was made instrumental to the Convincement of many. He was very serviceable and successful in accommodating Differences amongst his Neighbours; and having frequent Access to Persons of high Rank in Life, he was thereby very useful not only to remove Prejudices from their Minds, by opening the Doctrines and Principles most surely believed among us, but in obtaining their friendly Regard and Assistance when Occasion required: Thus he spent a long and useful Life, through many close Trials and Afflictions which attended him both within and without, he bore all with Steadiness and Resignation, and his Memory and Understanding were preserved to the Admiration of many who knew him.

Some Lines he wrote, about sixteen Years before his Decease, seem to describe the State of his Mind in succeeding Years, viz.

" I am now waiting, and beseeching God
" Almighty to grant me the Continuance of
" his blessed Grace and Holy Spirit, to aid
" and assist me for a full Preparation for
" Death, and calmly to resign myself to it;
" and above all, to grant me his Aid in that

" painful

" painful and trying Seafon, that I may
" for ever praife his Holy Name, who is
" for ever worthy with his dear Son, who
" is my dear and bleffed Saviour, *Amen.*"

He departed this Life at his Houfe in *Kendall*, the 30th of the Twelfth Month 1769, and was interred in Friends Burial-ground the 1ft of the Firft Month 1770. Aged ninety-two, a Minifter upwards of fixty Years.

DANIEL STANTON, of the City of *Philadelphia*, was born in that City about the Year 1708: His Father dying before his Birth, and his Mother a few Years after, he fuffered great Trial and Hardfhips when very young ; but being early concern'd to feek the Knowledge of God, he had a fervent Defire to attend religious Meetings, tho' fubjected to many Difficulties and Difcouragements before that Privilege was allowed him ; yet being earneft in his Defires to obtain Divine Favour, he was eminently fupported under great Conflicts and Probations, and continuing faithful to the Degrees of Light and Grace communicated, a Difpenfation of the Gofpel-Miniftry was committed to him fome Time before the Term of of his Apprenticeſhip was expired ; and abiding under the ſanctifying Power of Truth, he grew in his Gift and became a zealous and faithful Miniſter.

And though he was very exemplary in his Induſtry and Diligence, in labouring faithfully at his Trade to provide for his own Support, and after he married and had Children for their Maintenance, and was often concern'd to adviſe others to the ſame neceſſary Care ; yet he continued fervent in Spirit for the Promotion of Truth and Righteouſneſs, ſo that he was ſoon engaged to leave Home, and the neareſt Connections of Nature, to publiſh the Glad-tidings of the Goſpel, frequently viſiting the Meetings of Friends in the Province of *Pennſilvania* and the adjacent Provinces, and ſeveral Times as far as the Eaſtern Parts of *New-England*.

In the Year 1748, in Company with *Samuel Nottingham*, he viſited the few Meetings in the Iſland of *Barbadoes*, and by the Way of *Antigua* to *Tortola*, where after ſtaying ſome Time, they embarked for *Europe*. Their Voyage thither was attended with ſome ſingular Hazards and Danger, which occaſioned their Landing in *Ireland*, where after he had viſited the Meetings of Friends he embarked for *England*, and viſited the

the Meetings generally in *Great-Britain* to the Comfort and Satisfaction of Friends; his meek, circumfpect Conduct and Converfation, and lively edifying Miniftry, rendring his Vifits very acceptable and his Memory precious.

After his Return to his native Country he vifited Friends in all the Southern Provinces as far as *South-Carolina*, and about two Years before his Death the Families of Friends in fome Parts of *Weft-Jerfey*, the City of *New-York* and *Long-Ifland*; he return'd from this Service with great Peace and Satisfaction, expreffing his Apprehenfion, *That he was now clear of all Places, and that his Stay here was near over, having an Evidence that he had been faithfully concern'd from his Youth to fear and ferve God.*

When at Home he was much employ'd in vifiting the Sick and Afflicted, to whom he adminiftred his fpiritual Advice and Experience, and was often engaged in humble Prayer for their Support; and in the diftributing to the Neceffitous according to his Circumftances, he manifefted his benevolent Difpofition. His Love to the rifing Generation was very great, which he manifefted by his affectionate Notice of them, and efpecially of thofe who were religioufly inclined,

clined, his House being open to receive such.
And his Concern was great, *That those who
had the Glad-tidings of the Gospel to publish,
might be true Examples to the Flock, and adorn
the Doctrine they had to deliver by a circum-
spect Life and Conversation.*

On the 5th Day of the Fifth Month 1770,
he was violently seized with the *Billious Cholic*,
and continued in great Pain for several Days,
but being somewhat easier he attended two
Meetings on the First-day, in which he was
much favour'd in his publick Ministry, and
expressed, *That he thought his Time would
not be long.* He was enabled to attend the
Monthly-meeting at *Philadelphia* the 25th
of the said Month, which was the last publick
Meeting he was at, being the next Morning
seized with a renewed Attack of the same
Disorder, which increased on him for several
Days ; yet through all he was mercifully
supported in much Resignation and Patience,
rather inclining, if it was the Lord's Will,
to be released.

During the Time of his Sickness, he often
expressed his Concern lest his Friends should
be too anxious for his Recovery, saying, *If
he should live longer and through any human
Frailty or Infirmity occasion any Reproach, it
would be Cause of Sorrow to them.* The
Evening

Evening of the First-day before he died, several Friends coming to see him, he spoke a considerable Time to them, having before been desirous of such an Opportunity of the Company of his Friends, to set down and wait on God, which was his great Delight. The Evening before he died, he expressed to his Friend *Israel Pemberton*, who sat up with him, his great Thankfulness, *That his Head was preserved from Pain, and his Understanding clear ; and that tho' it had been a Time of close Trial and deep Probation, he could say he felt the Evidence of Divine Support to attend him.*

He died the 28th of the Sixth Month 1770, in the sixty-second Year of his Age and forty-third of his Ministry, and the next Day his Body attended by a large Number of People of divers religious Denominations, after a Meeting being held for that Purpose, was interred in Friends Burial-ground in that City.

N. B. For a further Account of this Friend, see the Testimony given by the Monthly-meeting of *Philadelphia* of him, prefixed to his Journal, printed at *Philadelphia* in the Year 1772.

ELIZABETH

ELIZABETH ATKINSON, of *Milden-Hall* in *Suffolk*, was the Daughter of *Edward* and *Elizabeth Peachy*, of the fame Place, Friends well efteemed, who gave this their Daughter a religious Education ; and while very young, fhe was favoured with a Divine Vifitation, and yielding Obedience to the Heavenly Vifion, fhe became qualified for her Mafter's Ufe, and receiv'd a Gift in the Miniftry about the twenty-fecond Year of her Age. She was faithfully concerned to yield Obedience to the Manifeftations of Duty, in which fhe experienced Peace.

When about thirty fhe join'd in Marriage with *Samuel Atkinfon,* a Friend of the fame Meeting, and fome few Years after it pleafed the Lord to try her in a clofe Manner, by diffolving this very near and dear Connexion : Thus being left a Widow with fix young Children and in low Circumftances : This Difpenfation of Heaven was attended with Baptifms and Exercifes on many Accounts, her Situation being fuch that fhe found it neceffary to ufe unwearied Diligence for the Support of her Family, not willing to be burthenfome, but having a few Things, was

Z · therewith

therewith content. It does not feem her Family, whofe Neceffity fhe ever appear'd to have due Regard to, hindred her in her Gofpel-Labours ; but fhe was obedient to the Requirings and Manifeftations of Duty, faithfully giving up to go on the Lord's Errands.

At the awful Approach of the undeniable Meffenger of Death, fhe poffeffed a quiet Compofure of Soul, often wifhing *to be diffolved, to be with Chrift* ; yet humbly waiting the Lord's Time for the Accomplifhment of his Will, and being full of Days and full of Peace, fhe was greatly favoured to very near the End of her Time, fenfible and lively, and was frequently engaged to exprefs, *The Lord's Goodnefs to her had been great and wonderful* ; earneftly recommending to thofe who vifited her, *To ferve him faithfully*, and in an efpecial Manner to the Youth, *To dedicate the Bud and Bloffom of their Days to him, for that they could not ferve a better Mafter.*

A fhort Time before her Death, finding her Mind very low, was fearful fhe had offended ; earneft were her Cries unto the Lord, *That fhe might not depart under a Cloud*, which he gracioufly anfwered by the renewing of his Love, and lifting up of his glori-

ous

ous Countenance, so that she broke forth in the following Words, *Glory, Honour and high Renown be given to him, who wears the Heavenly Crown. The Lord is my Reward, and at his Right-hand are Rivers of Pleasure, and that for evermore.*

She departed this Life the 3d of the Seventh Month 1770, and was buried in Friends Burial-ground at *Milden-Hall*, the 8th of the same. Aged eighty-eight, a Minister sixty-six Years.

THOMAS MAWDITT, of *Cullumpton* in the County of *Devon*, was educated in the Way of the Church of *England*, and about the twentieth Year of his Age was convinced of the blessed Truth. By the Accounts receiv'd of him, he appear'd in the Ministry about the thirty-third Year of his Age, and his Services therein were acceptable. He was a diligent Attender of Meetings, tho' of an infirm Constitution of Body; of an exemplary Conduct among Men, and of an innocent Deportment.

Having left behind him a Narrative in Manuscript of his Convincement, the following is a Copy of it, *viz.*

" Some

" Some Paſſages of my Life having of
" late been brought freſh in my Remem-
" brance, I thought proper to commit them
" to Writing, that others might ſee the
" great Love of God, in Chriſt, to my
" Soul, and be encouraged to follow on to
" know and obey him.

" While I was young and tender in Years,
" the Lord was pleaſed to put his Fear into
" my Heart, which was to me the Beginning
" of Wiſdom, becauſe it made me careful
" both of my Words and Actions ; and ſo
" long as I kept upon my Watch againſt
" Sin, the Lord gave me true Peace and
" Quietude of Mind, but when I was un-
" watchful, the Tempter often prevailed
" with his Temptations, which brought the
" righteous Judgments of God upon my
" Soul, and made me cry unto him for
" Mercy and Forgiveneſs ; and the Lord
" was gracious to me, and forgave me
" Time after Time as I repented of the
" Evil, ſo that I can from my own Expe-
" rience ſay, *That there is Mercy with the*
" *Lord that he may be feared* ; and thus he
" gave me Strength to call upon him while
" he was near, and to ſeek him while he
" was to be found. He was near in Spirit,
" reproving me for my Sins, altho' I then
" knew him not ; and in this State I often
" made

" made Covenant, *That if the Lord would*
" *forgive me, then I would live more watchful*
" *than I had hitherto* ; but as it was made'
" in my own Will it was foon broken, and'
" I was ftill under the Adminiftration of
" Condemnation ; the Senfe thereof often
" made me cry unto God, *That he would de-*
" *liver me from the Body of this Death* ; for
" in this State, when I would do Good,
" Evil was prefent with me, and I did the
" Things I would not ; and finding myfelf
" overcome Time after Time, notwith-'
" ftanding my Endeavours to the contrary;
" I was ready to conclude that there was no
" living without Sin in the World, although
" I found it a Burthen too heavy to bear.

" About this Time I began to think what
" People to join with, for I was not fatisfied
" in the Way I was in, and I befought the
" moft high God, *That he would direct me*
" *what People to join with* ; and while I
" was under this Concern of Mind, on a
" Firft-day of the Week, as I was walking
" to the Place of Worfhip in Company
" with two of the People called *Quakers*,
" one of them afked me to go with them
" to their Meeting, adding, that there were
" to be two Strangers there that Day ; and
" I accordingly went, and after we had
" fitten fome Time in Silence, one of them
" ftood

" ſtood up and ſpoke, after that the other ;
" I do not remember much of what they
" ſaid, but it appeared to me that their
" Preaching was like that of the Apoſtles,
" and that they were enabled by a Meaſure
" of the ſame Spirit and a Degree of the
" ſame Power ; and I alſo felt ſuch a Mea-
" ſure of that Spirit and Power which helped
" them in their Miniſtry as I never enjoyed
" before ; and it was to me a Day of Glad-
" tidings of great Joy, and my Soul did
" magnify the Lord, and my Spirit rejoiced
" in God my Saviour.

" This gave me a full Satisfaction of
" Mind what People to join with, altho' at
" firſt it did look ſtrange to me to ſee a
" People ſit in Silence as they did, for I
" had been feeding upon Words, until I
" was directed unto Chriſt, the Word nigh
" in the Heart, and to know him to be my
" Teacher : Thus the Lord brought me off
" from a Man-made Miniſtry unto the Mi-
" niſter of the Sanctuary and true Taber-
" nacle, which God hath pitched and not
" Man, everlaſting Praiſe be given to his
" Name. Here the Lord brought me into
" a State of Silence, out of my formal
" Prayers and Will-worſhip, to wait upon
" him, until he was pleaſed to help me to
" pray with the Spirit and with Underſtand-
" ing ;

" ing ; but when he was pleafed to fhew
" me that I muft ufe the fingular Number,
" as Thou and Thee to one Perfon, it was
" as Death to me, for I faw I fhould be
" defpifed and rejected ; and here I found
" in degree that Crofs which the Apoftle
" fpoke of, *that crucified to the World, and
" the World unto him* ; and until I knew my
" own Will in meafure flain, I was not able
" to ufe it ; but when I did ufe it, after I
" believed it was required of me, I had
" great Peace of Mind ; and if at any Time
" I did not ufe it for Fear of offending Man,
" I was under Condemnation and Trouble
" of Mind until I did ufe it without Refpect
" of Perfons : I know it was the Lord's
" Doing, for I did it not in Imitation but
" by Revelation. Neither could I any more
" pull off my Hat and bow to any Man :
" And thus the Lord led me Step by Step
" into Obedience unto him ; and as long as
" I lived in Obedience to what he was
" pleafed to manifeft unto me, I reaped
" that Peace and Joy in the Holy Ghoft,
" that all the Favour and Friendfhip of
" Men are not to be compared with. About
" this Time a Concern came upon my Mind
" to bear a publick Teftimony in Meetings
" to the Truth, which made me both to
" fear and tremble ; whereupon I let in the
" Reafoner, and looked into my own Weak-
" nefs

" nefs as a Man, and how unfit I was for
" fo great a Work as the Work of the
" Miniftry ; when I fhould have looked
" unto the Lord, who is able to ftrengthen
" the Weak and confirm the Feeble-minded,
" and which I had in Times paft witneffed
" to my Comfort : Here it was I loft my
" Peace and Quiet which I had in a State of
" Obedience, for I went from the true Wit-
" nefs within, even the Spirit of Truth,
" which did and would have led me into
" all Truth, and I joined with the Rea-
" foner, and fo erred and went aftray from
" the Way of the Lord as a loft Sheep :
" Here the Enemy of Mankind got Advan-
" tage upon me, and I could not ftand
" faithfully in my Teftimony for the Truth
" as I formerly had, but grew weaker and
" weaker, and was toffed with a Tempeft
" and not comforted ; yet in this forrowful
" State I fometimes had a little Hope that
" the Lord would deliver me, which was
" fome Stay to my Mind, and I was made
" to cry, *Lord ! if thou flay me yet will I*
" *truft in thee* ; and I would often pray
" unto God, *That he would reftore me again,*
" *and that if it did pleafe him to bring the*
" *like Concern upon me any more, I would*
" *be faithful and obedient to his Requirings* ;
" but this I could not attain unto, which
" brought me very low in my Mind, and I
" was

" was almoft ready to defpair, for I found
" myfelf fo hardened that I could not la-
" ment my State and Condition as formerly,
" fo that I was afraid the Day of my Vifita-
" tion was over, and when all Hope feemed
" to be loft the Word of the Lord was
" unto me, *As thou haft gradually fallen,*
" *fo thou fhalt gradually rife* ; which had fo
" good Effect as to bring with it a living
" Hope, that was as an Anchor to my Soul,
" ftedfaft and fure, and preferved my Mind
" from being carried away with the Floods
" of Temptation, which were many and
" great in thofe Days, that it was through
" Faith in Chrift, the Word nigh in the
" Heart, which I found to be quick and
" powerful, that I came to be reftored
" again in due Time, unto a State of Obe-
" dience ; and the Lord now favoured me
" with many good Meetings, which made
" me often defire for the Meeting-time,
" for in my filent Waiting upon him, I
" found my Strength renewed : After this
" it was fhewn me that I muft alter the
" Place of my Sitting, and one Day as the
" Meeting-time drew on, I prayed to God
" in my Heart, *That he would favour me*
" *with a good Meeting* ; but the Anfwer
" was, *If thou doft not go and fit in that*
" *Place, how canft thou expect a good Meet-*

A a   " ing ?

" *ing?* For until now I was not come to a
" Refolution ; but now when the Meeting-
" time came, I went and fat in the Place
" fhewed me, not knowing further what
" might be required of me, and after fome
" Time of Silence I found a Concern of
" Mind to fpeak unto the People as follow-
" eth : *There is a Seed of God amongft you,*
" *but it lieth oppreffed,* &c.

" And now I can fay after many Years
" Experience, *Hitherto the Lord has helped*
" *me, and he is not a hard Mafter,* as fome
" flothful Servants have faid, *for he doth*
" *not gather where he hath not ftrowed,*
" *neither reap where he hath not fown* ; but
" all that are born of that Seed which is
" incorruptible, and of the Word of God
" which liveth and abideth for ever, can fay,
" *There is no Condemnation to them that are*
" *in Chrift Jefus, who walk not after the*
" *Flefh, but after the Spirit* ; *for the Law*
" *of the Spirit of Life hath made them free*
" *from the Law of Sin and Death.* And
" here in brief have I fhewn what the Lord
" hath done for my Soul, for it is he that
" hath plucked my Feet out of the miry
" Clay, and fet them upon a Rock that was
" higher than I ; wherefore to him fhall
" the Honour, Glory and Praife be given,
" who

" who is over all worthy for ever and ever-
" more.
" *Signed* T. M. 1748."

In his laſt Ilneſs, his Underſtanding and
Senſes were preſerved, and he expreſſed his
being refreſhed in his Spirit, and as he found
his End approaching he frequently deſired,
*If agreeable to the Will of the Almighty, that
he might be releaſed, under a well-grounded
Apprehenſion that his Day's Work was done.*

He departed this Life the 13th of the
Seventh Month 1770. Aged eighty-one,
and had been a Miniſter about forty-eight
Years.

SARAH WAGSTAFFE, of
Chipping-Norton in *Oxfordſhire*, Widow
of *Thomas Wagſtaffe*, formerly of *Banbury*
in the ſame County, was born in the Year
1695, and educated in the Way of Truth,
in the City of *London*, where her Parents
lived ; and being faithful to the Dictates
thereof in her young Years, ſhe experienced
its ſupporting Influence under many Exerciſes
which fell to her Lot through Life, having
often to remark to her Children, the Benefit
thereof ; and by ſuitable Inſtructions endea-
A a 2   vour'd

vour'd to lead their Minds to regard its Dictates when very young, and when remote from her was often by Writing, reviving suitable Counsel to them, being herself a good Example, a tender Parent, and well beloved among her Neighbours and Friends.

Towards the Decline of her Life she was afflicted with bodily Weaknefs, which confined her to her Chamber for fome Months before she died, which she bore with much Refignation and Patience; often defiring she might hold out to the End, which she patiently waited for. Before she became incapable, she employ'd her Pen to fuch of her Children as were at a Diftance from her, particularly to one of her Sons, when she by Letter took her laft Leave of him and his Family, she expreffed herfelf thus:

" That my Children and Grand-children " may be fo conducted through Mutability " as we may all meet in Joy and Blifs, I " entreat," fays she, " in Love, that thou- " and thine may mind your future State " above all, and let not the Hurrys of this " tranfitory World, with all its tinfel Glare, " Pride, Grandeur and Vanity, choak the " good Seed, which as it is permitted to " take Root, will bring forth the good " Fruit, which will entitle you to Difciple- " fhip,

" fhip, and give you a Beauty and Glory
" which all thefe Things cannot give.

" Dear Son, be on thy Guard and watch
" over thy Children ; reprefs all Pride,
" Ambition, and vain Converfation in them
" as much as poffible. O this World's
" fading Enjoyments has over-run the major
" Part of our Society ! How few live up
" to what they profefs ! I write with a fer-
" vent Defire for all your immortal Souls,
" each of which is of more Value than all
" this World, which with all its checker'd
" Pleafures and Afflictions muft foon end
" as the Bubble on the Water, and then
" Peace with our Maker will only ftand us
" inftead."

At another Time, when to Appearance
fhe grew near her End, fhe expreffed herfelf
to this Effect : *That her Truft and Dependance was on her almighty Protector, Saviour
and Redeemer, by whofe Grace fhe doubted
not, but that fhe fhould clofe in Peace.*

After which fhe continued fome Weeks,
in much Quietnefs and Patience, until the
5th of the Firft Month 1771, when fhe
quietly departed without Sigh or Groan,
and was interred in Friends Burial-ground at
Chipping-Norton aforefaid, after a folemn
Meeting,

Meeting, the 13th of the fame. Aged near feventy-fix Years.

_____

ABRAHAM SHACKLETON, born at *Harden* in the Parifh of *Bingley, Yorkfhire*, according to the beft Information was the youngeft Child of *Richard* and *Sarah Shackleton* of that Place. His Mother died when he was about fix Years of Age, his Father when he was about eight. Tho' deprived fo early of religious Parents, the Impreffion made by their careful Education of him was not in vain ; he ufed often to commemorate the tender Care and Concern of his pious Father, how he followed him (his Son) when very young to his Bed-fide, and on leaving him to his Repofe, awfully recommended him to feek the Divine Blefling. And this Blefling did remarkably attend him during the Courfe of his Life : When very young and expofed to manifold Dangers in his Education afterwards, this Blefling followed him, and by its precious Influence, led him afide from his Companions, and in folitary Places, to feek the Lord, and to witnefs the Operation of his Hand.

His Employment being that of a School-mafter, he labour'd in it with confcientious Care

Care for many Years; in which he had not only the Education of Children of the Members of our own Society, but alfo fome of various Denominations, fome of whom fill confpicuous Stations in the World, and retain an affectionate Regard for his Memory; and from a Remembrance of his Diligence and Care in their Tuition, his living Example of Uprightnefs, Temperance and Humility, a great Regard for the Society.

And altho' in this arduous Employment he met with many Probations, yet keeping to a feeling Senfe of Divine Support, he grew from Strength to Strength, and became a very ufeful and valuable Member of the Society; and in the Station of an Elder, had often to minifter in his own Houfe, in the Families of Friends, and in the Church, in which Counfel dropt from him in much Tendernefs and Sweetnefs.

Thus through a Courfe of many Years, he was conducted in great Circumfpection in a living Travail for the Profperity of Truth, and that the Profeffors of it might be preferved out of hurtful Things; had frequently to teftify againft fuch Superfluities as fometimes came in his Way, particularly a Practice too prevalent among many, that of fitting long after Dinner with Bottles and
Glaffes

Glaſſes before them, as having a Tendency to draw into many Snares.

He was alſo much concerned at a Cuſtom too prevalent among Friends, of uncovering the Head by way of Ceremony upon entering into a Room, and was pained when he ſaw the Youth or others in that Practice : He uſed to ſay, that when he was a young Man, he durſt not baulk his Teſtimony in that Reſpect, though the Croſs occaſioned thereby ſeemed as bitter as Death.

After a diligent Diſcharge of his laborious Employment for many Years, he became in a greater degree ſeparated from the Cares of this Life, and devoted much of his Time in attending Meetings for Diſcipline in various Parts of the Nation of *Ireland*, where he was ſettled in his School, and alſo the Yearly-meeting in *London*, to the Help of his Brethren and his own Peace.

After the Death of his Wife, who had been his beloved and faithful Helpmeet many Years, and who departed this Life in cheerful Reſignation, great Compoſure and ſweet Peace, in the eightieth Year of her Age, he quitted Houſe-keeping and retired to live with a Relation in the ſame Village where he was viſited with his laſt Ilneſs,

Ilnefs, which he bore with great Patience, faying, *He was mercifully dealt with.*

During the Courfe of his Diforder and while able, he got out to Meetings, and when render'd incapable thereof, many Friends vifited him, to whom he was drawn forth in fweet Counfel to the tendering of their Spirits : Many were the feafonable Opportunities of this Sort, and many fenfible favoury Expreffions dropt from him, which fhewed his Mind was often replenifhed with Heavenly Oil.

A little before his Departure, he faid to his Relations about him, *I have no Caufe to grieve, neither would I have you* ; yet mentioned, *He had nothing to truft to but the Mercies of the Almighty.* His Mind was often favoured with Heavenly Joy, and one Night after much Pain, he expreffed with a melodious Voice, *I am well, I feel no Pain, I feel Good. O the Elders ! the Elders ! they fhould dig for the arifing of the Well of Life as with the Staves in their Hands. Spring up, O Well, and I will fing unto thee !* At another Time, in a Manner fimilar to this, he uttered thefe Words, *Thofe that are faithful to the End fhall receive a Crown, a Crown that fadeth not away ; but Rebellion is as the Sin of Witchcraft.*

B b   Much

Much more dropt from him, but not being taken down, could not be perfectly remembered.

He departed in great Peace, the 24th of the Sixth Month 1771, and was interred the 27th of the fame. Aged feventy-four Years.

JOSEPH BEVINGTON, Son of *Timothy* and *Hannah Bevington*, of the City of *Worcefter*, was a young Man, who from a Child was fober and well-inclined, exemplary in his Conduct, dutiful to his Parents, and of a tender and loving Difpofition ; and as he grew up towards Man's Eftate, gave evident Proofs of a fuitable Attention to that Divine Principle in his own Mind, by which his Conduct was fo regulated, as to give Ground of Hope he would fill up his Station with Reputation to himfelf and Comfort to all his Friends.

He was taken ill about the 1ft of the Sixth Month 1771, and his Diforder gradually increafing, his Father found his Mind engaged to go and fit by him one Evening on his going to Bed fooner than ufual, and in much Tendernefs expreffed, That though he had
hoped,

hoped, he might, in the Appointment of Providence, have been his Succeffor, both in the Church and in the World ; yet when Illnefs attacked (even one fo young and healthy as him) the Iffue might be doubtful, and therefore defired him to examine his Accounts and Meetnefs for a final Change, if the Lord fhould pleafe to remove him. He, in affectionate lively Terms, expreffed the Senfe he had of his Father's tender Regard for him, and they parted that Evening under a fweet Senfe of that Love which unites beyond the Ties of Nature.

His Diftemper increafing, which proved to be a *Fever*, he was mercifully preferved fenfible ; his Father and Mother being often concerned to wait on the Lord by his Bed-fide, he was frequently broken into Tendernefs, but did not fay much.

Getting a little better, he went into the Country for the Air ; in fome Converfation with a Friend there who was in a declining State, he expreffed, *That he did not know how it might pleafe Providence to deal with him ; but,* faid he, *I had rather, if confiftent with his Will, go now, than live longer and fall into any thing that might bring Difhonour to our Holy Profeffion.*

A near

A near Friend visiting him, found him in Tears, and expressing her Fears least any thing had grieved him, he answered, *No, but he was looking towards another World.*

He returned out of the Country in about a Week rather poorly, and on the Morrow was seized with a shivering Fit, and sending for his Father, he with Earnestness took him by the Hand, and said, *Dear Father, I have already gone through a very trying Time, but I believe this will be much more so ;* and expressing his Care for his Parents, added, *He that made me has a Right to take me away when he pleases ; and I desire as he hath favoured me with much Resignation of Mind to his Will hitherto, it may continue. I have not always been so careful and circumspect in my Conduct as I ought to have been ; but lately, and especially since my Illness, I don't know that I could have done better, and trust it will be well with me.*

His Indisposition increasing, all Hopes of his Recovery was removed, in which, he being in extream Pain and Sickness, his Parents were engaged to wait on the Lord with him, who was graciously pleased to comfort their Minds ; and under this broken, humble, contrite State before him (who sustains his People in every needful Time) this beloved

loved Youth with an audible Voice, faid, *O what a dreadful Day would this have been to me, if I had Cause to fear I was going to meet an angry Judge, that might fay, Depart from me thou Worker of Iniquity! But,* faid he, *I have Hope in God, that I shall be admitted into his Reft.* Which much bowed the Hearts of all his near Connexions prefent, and helped to bear up their Spirits in that trying Seafon ; and foon after this dear Object of paternal Affection quietly departed this Life in his Father's Arms, having, in a good Degree, efcaped the Dangers, Jeopardies and Temptations attendant on human Life, and we truft was gathered with the Beauty of Innocency upon him, to the Juft of all Generations, in the twenty-firft Year of his Age, on the 9th of the Seventh Month 1771, and was buried in the City of *Worcefter* on the 14th of the fame.

ANN GURNEY, Daughter of *John* and *Ann Gurney*, of the City of *Norwich*, was a comely Perfon, of quick Parts, and a lively Turn. Hence fhe early fhewed a natural Inclination to Height and Gaiety, which brought a Concern upon her Parents on her Account, left fhe fhould be carried away with the common Stream into Liberties

[190]

Liberties of an hurtful Nature. But such was the gracious Dealing of Divine Mercy towards her, that, some Time before she was taken with her last Ilness, an agreeable Alteration was observed in her Disposition and Conduct, which undoubtedly arose from the cordial Reception she had given to an Heavenly Visitation upon her Spirit ; for, in the Sequel, it evidently appeared, a State of Preparation was thereby effected, properly to endure the tedious Ilness and solemn Event that ensued.

For many Months, her usual State of Health seemed, at Times, to be broke in upon, and Tokens of Infirmity appeared, which increased upon her, and at length terminated in a settled Decline.

Several Weeks before her Decease, she chearfully said to her Sisters, *My little Tenement is much shaken, and will soon be in Decay.* A while after, her Mother saying, She should be very thankful if it pleased Providence to raise her up again ; she replied, *That must be as it pleases Providence ; but I can never go with less Guilt.*

She said, *She believed Divine Goodness had often been very near to her, and supported her ; for she could not have supported herself.*

To

To her Sister *Lucy*, she said, *My dear, I hope thou wilt never do any thing to grieve thy Father and Mother, and be sure do nothing against thy own Conscience. Don't grieve for me ; for tho' we have loved one another, it is right we should part.*

She acknowledged, *She had sometimes gone contrary to the Testimony of her Conscience ; but she had known Sorrow for it, and she believed, Forgiveness ; and made no Doubt, but if it pleased Providence to take her away, she should go to Heaven.*

To her Mother, she said, *I know it will be a Loss, make it but a little one.* Her Mother replying; It is a bitter Cup, my Dear ; she answered, *But Providence will sweeten the bitter Cup.* And on her Mother's saying, She believed a glorious Mansion was prepared for her ; she replied with much Earnestness, *I make no Doubt of that, and I expect to see thee and my Father there.*

Desiring her Sisters to be called, she told them, *She was glad to see them* ; and laying a While sweetly still, she awfully said, *She hoped they would always live in the Fear of the Lord, and never do any thing against their Consciences.*

Being

Being told her Uncle *Edmund Gurney*, said, That she was in a sweet Frame, and compared her to Mount *Sion*, that could not be moved; she answered, *Then why does my Mother grive so?*

Her Father going one Morning into her Chamber, she desired him to come by her Bed-side, saying, *She was glad to see him, and that she thought herself not worse.* On his saying, *He hoped her better Parent, her Heavenly Father, had been near to her that Night;* she answered, *Yes, that he has, and I hope near thee too.*

Two Days before her Decease, she earnestly prayed, *The Lord would be with her to the End, and give her Patience to the last; and that, if he pleased, he would mercifully grant her an easy Passage, as her Uncle* Edmund *had prayed for on her Account.* She declared, *She was very willing to go,* with many other comfortable Expressions.

She was composed and easy in her Mind throughout her long and painful Illness, and never once expressed a Wish to live. She said, *She had many near and dear Relations to leave; but she should not know the Pain of losing them.*

Thus

Thus having shewn a steady Example of
Faith, Patience, Resignation, and Heavenly
Compofure, in the Bloom of Youth, she
departed the 19th of the First Month 1772.
Aged fourteen Years and nine Months.

WILLIAM HUNT, of New-
Gordon in the Province of North
Carolina in America, was born in the Province
of Pennfilvania ; and by Accounts received
he was first reached by Truth about the
eighth Year of his Age, which continued to
follow him from Time to Time, that when
in Company with his Acquaintance, he has
been often tendered and led to feek folitary
Places to vent his Tears ; altho' he then did
not know what it was that fo broke in upon
his Spirit.

Being fituated in a Part at that early Period
of his Life, where no Religion prevailed,
but the People lived rather diffolutely, he
had no one to tell the Diftrefs and Exercife
of his Mind to (for his Mother dying when
he was young, who he had been inform'd
was a religious Woman, and his Father when
he was about twelve, he was left quite alone.)
But after fome Time going to live with his
Sifter, and thofe tender Impreffions continu-

C c   ing,

ing, the Lord in Mercy ſhewed him, *They were from the immediate Operation of his own Spirit, and that his Growth in Truth and Experience of its pure Virtue, lay in his being faithful to the Dictates thereof*; by which he was fitted for Service, even in very early Years, his Mouth being open'd in Teſtimony before he was fifteen Years of Age; and through the Heavenly Influence of the Spirit, he became an able Miniſter, rightly dividing the Word of Truth, to the great Comfort and Edification of the Church where his Lot was caſt.

He was concern'd to travel in Truth's Service before his twentieth Year, and viſited the Provinces of *Virginia* and *Maryland*; and afterwards in the Courſe of his *Chriſtian* Progreſs, all the Provinces of *America*, and almoſt all the Meetings therein. And altho' he had a large Family, whoſe Subſiſtance much depended on his Induſtry and Care; yet, when he found the Requirings of Truth, and became fully ſatisfied thereof, he chearfully gave up all into the Care of that Hand which drew him into Service, relying thereon for the Preſervation of himſelf and all his, in every Diſpenſation of Providence, and which was mercifully afforded to him.

In

In the Year 1771 he came to this Nation on a religious Visit, and travelled through most Parts of the North of *England*, *Scotland* and *Ireland*, and after the Yearly-meeting 1772, he visited the general Quarterly-meetings at *Colchester*, *Woodbridge* and *Norwich*; soon after which he proceeded thro' *Lincolnshire* for *Hull*, whence with his Companion *Thomas Thornbrugh*, our Friend *Samuel Emlin*, jun. of *Philadelphia*, and *Morris Birkbeck*, he embarked for *Holland*; and after visiting the few Friends there, he embarked in a Vessel bound to *Scarborough*, but by contrary Winds landed at *Shields* the latter End of the Eighth Month, with a Dedication of Heart for further Service if required; but was soon after he landed taken ill of the *Small Pox*. In the Course of which Ilness, his Mind was preserved perfectly calm, and his Patience and Fortitude were truly great, as was also his Resignation to Divine Disposal, signifying to his Companion, *That his coming there was providential, but that his Sickness was nigh unto Death, if not quite*; for, says he, *when I wait, I seem inclosed, I see no farther*.

To a Friend who remarked, That what ever Affliction we may be tried with, we may yet see Cause of Thankfulness, he replied, *Great Cause indeed, I never saw it*

C c 2

clearer ; *O the Wisdom, the Wisdom and Goodness, the Mercy and Kindness has appeared to me wonderful! And the further and deeper we go, the more we wonder* ; *I have admired since I was cast on this Bed, that all the World does not seek after the Enjoyment of Truth, it so far transcends all other Things.*

At another Time, to some Friends who came to see him, he said, *The Lord knows how I have loved you from our first Acquaintance, and longed for your Growth and Establishment in the blessed Truth, and I now feel the same renewed afresh* ; adding, *He much desired they might fill up their Places Providence intended, and lay up Treasure in Heaven* ; *for,* says he, *what would a thousand Worlds avail me now.* He also expressed his Satisfaction, *He had not spent his Time idly since he came to* England, *nor neglected one Meeting he could well attend, and that under so great a Load of bodily Affliction, what a Treasure a quiet Mind was.*

At another Time, he said with great Composure, *The Lord knows best, I am in his Hand, let him do what he will* ; and leaning on *Morris Birkbeck,* he said, *Dear* Morris, *I have a Request to make, which is, in Case I am suddenly taken away, do thou write to my dear Wife, and let her know All's well* ; *write also*

also to my Children, to improve the Hints I frequently gave for their Conduct while with them and since.

At another Time, a Day or two before his Death, he said to him, *This is a trying Time, but my Mind is above it all*; and it was observable that a sweet Melody was in his Heart when few Words were expressed.

A little before his Death, he said triumphantly, *Friends, Truth reigns over-all*; and soon after quietly departed this Life, the 9th of the Ninth Month 1772, and was interred in Friends Burial-ground at *Newcastle* upon *Tyne* the 11th of the same. Aged thirty-nine, a Minister twenty-four Years.

ELIZABETH SMITH, of *Burlington* in *West-Jersey* in *America*, was one whose Deportment from a Child was composed and steady; frequently while others sought Recreation and Amusements Abroad she chose to be at Home, employing herself in the Business of the Family, or improving her Mind by some useful Application. As she grew up, *the Reproofs of Instruction* became the Way of Life to her, and she was governed by a meek and quiet Spirit; her

Conversation

Converfation and Conduct feem'd to be almoft one continued Example of Child like Simplicity and Innocence. Her Mother dying while fhe was young, the Care of her Father's Family devolved upon her for a confiderable Time before his Death ; her Duty to him and Behaviour in general, gain'd the Love of a careful religious Parent, and a Bleffing attended her, as her future Life manifefted ; her Words were few, but favory and inftructive ; fhe had a feeling Heart, and the Diftreffed were often relieved by her Charity ; happy in herfelf, fhe endeavour'd to make all about her fo. She had a great Regard for the Holy Scriptures ; on taking up a Bible, fhe remarked to a particular Friend, what a Treafure it contained ; and fought to inculcate the Reading thereof, and to difcourage the fafhionable Books of the Times.

It was her Concern frequently to retire to wait on the Lord to know her Strength renew'd in him, and the Effects were vifible by a chearful Serenity on her Countenance.

In her early Youth fhe was called to the Work of the Miniftry, in which fhe deliver'd herfelf in a clear confiftent Manner ; and it flowing from the right Spring, was often attended with good Effect. She was concern'd cern'd to travel in the Exercise of her Gift as far to the Northward as *New-England*, and also to some of the Southern Provinces, and frequently to the Meetings about Home. But in her latter Time was greatly afflicted with a *Dropsical* Disorder, which subjected her to be tapped, by which she was so far relieved, that for several Years she had a better State of Health ; in which Interval she frequently attended Meetings for Worship and Discipline ; and the last Summer before her Death, though much enfeebled in Body, had often very acceptable Service in the Ministry, alive and strong in the best Sense, her Company was greatly satisfactory to Friends about her.

Her Disorder returning, she waited for her Change with a lively Hope ; and a Serenity of Mind attended her, being inwardly supported beyond mere human Attainment.

She uttered many Expressions during the Conflicts of her Illness, much to the Comfort and Satisfaction of those present. In solemn Supplication to the Almighty on her own Account, to be near and support her, she expressed herself in great Reverence to the following Effect : *Thou who art the God of my Life, who hast kept and fed me all my Life long, be now near and support by thy Presence,*

and

and if it is thy Will to put an End to my Being here, I submit: Be graciously pleased to give me Rest in thy Mansion, with thy dear Son, the Lamb immaculate, for ever and ever.

She often said, *She had nothing to do but to bear her Pains with Patience.* Once in great Extremity of Pain, she remarked that she had reasoned, *Why am I so afflicted? And had received this Answer in her Mind, My beloved Son, who never offended me, drank of the Cup before thee:* Thus, said she, *I am helped along with one kind Hint after another.* And she frequently expressed the Peace and Consolation she felt in those trying Moments, in having lived in the Fear of her Creator.

A Night or two before her Departure, she said, *She thought it easier for her to leave the World than for those who had Children to leave.* A near and intimate Friend replied, There were many who loved her: She said, *She did not know but it was so, and that Love would be consummated hereafter.* Towards the Conclusion, she said with great Tenderness of Spirit, *That she thought she was going;* and added, *I would not have you be troubled, it is to Joy unspeakable and full of Glory.*

She

She died the 2d of the Tenth Month 1772. Aged about forty-eight Years.

Among other of her Writings she left the following Epistle, which is thought meet to be here inferted, *viz.*

" *To the Quarterly and Monthly-meeting*
  " *of Women Friends, held at* Bur-
  " lington *and* Chesterfield *in* West
  " New Jersey *in* America.

  " *Dearly beloved Friends,*

" IN a fresh Remembrance of the many
" Seasons of Divine Favour, we have
" been made Partakers of together, in these
" Meetings appointed for transacting the
" Affairs of the Church, does my Spirit
" affectionately falute the Living : And not
" expecting to have the like Opportunity
" again, it rested with me to visit you after
" this Manner, with fervent Desires for the
" Prosperity of Truth and Righteousness in
" general ; and in a particular Manner, I
" have a Desire that our Sex may not fall
" short in living up to the faithful Perform-
" ance of their respective Duties, and dif-
D d   " charging

" charging that Truft which the Lord has
" committed to them honeftly, as in his
" Sight.   And for this great good End, I
" tenderly befeech you all, both Elder and
" Younger, that have known and may
" know the Mafter's Will concerning you,
" that you may be obedient.   Let not
" reafoning with Flefh and Blood, or plead-
" ing Excufes be Caufe of Unfitnefs (as you
" may think) prevail, and bear with me, if
" I obferve where that is the Cafe, Dwarfifh-
" nefs and Weaknefs will be the Confequence,
" and the beft Life is in Danger of being
" quite loft, as it may with Sorrow be
" remarked of fome who profefs with us,
" that a Name to live and be accounted as
" wife Virgins has feem'd to fuffice, whofe
" Cafe I have often lamented; and it is the
" ardent Prayer of my Soul for fuch, while
" I am writing this, that they may awake
" to Righteoufnefs, and diligently attend to
" the Teachings of the Spirit of the Lord,
" who will not fail to fit and qualify for
" every good Word and Work : And fatis-
" fied I am, as that becomes the principal
" Concern of Individuals, the Caufe of com-
" plaining of Mifconduct would be much
" removed, and our Zion would more
" confpicuoufly fhine, and there would be
" none found within her Walls barren or
" unfruitful in the faving Knowledge of
                                    " God ;

" God ; but that the ancient Promise made
" to Israel will remain to be the Portion of
" his People for ever, *That he would be as*
" *the Dew of* Hermon, *and as the Dew that*
" *descended upon the Mountains of* Zion,
" *for there the Lord commanded the Blessing,*
" *even Life for evermore,* Pf. cxxxiii. 3.

" And my dear young Friends, with
" Love unfeigned do I affectionately salute
" you, whose Company in these Meetings I
" have been glad of ; and I would encourage
" all who have a Right to Memberſhip, to
" the ſteady Attendance of them at the ſet
" Time, as often as you can while Health
" permits ; we are by Nature very ſhort
" ſighted, and know not when the Times
" of Refreſhment may come from the Pre-
" ſence of the Lord ; and therefore it's good
" for us to endeavour patiently to wait and
" quietly to hope for his Salvation, which
" I fully believe he is about to reveal in
" your Hearts ; and if you are faithful to
" the Diſcoveries of Divine Grace, your
" Underſtandings will be more and more
" opened in the Myſteries of God's King-
" dom, even that which was hid from Ages
" and Generations, and as the Apoſtle teſti-
" fies, is now revealed by the Spirit of the
" dear Son of God, our Holy Advocate
" with the Father.

" I have

" I have hinted above and hope shall die
" in the Faith of it, that the Lord will form
" a People to himself, that shall shew forth
" his Praise, and will yet beautify the House
" of his Glory ; under this Prospect my
" Spirit is at Times deeply bowed in Inter-
" cession for the Descendants of faithful
" Friends, that they may not render them-
" selves unworthy of so great a Mercy, and
" other especial Favours that they are blessed
" with beyond many ; but that they may
" not only be the called, but chosen of the
" Lord. Now in a Degree of my Hea-
" venly Father's Love, do I affectionately
" bid you farewel, desiring that Grace,
" Mercy and Peace may be multiplied in
" and amongst you, and conclude your true
" Friend,

" ELIZABETH SMITH.

" Burlington, the 30th of the
" Third Month 1772."

PRISCILLA

PRISCILLA GURNEY, Wife of *Edmund Gurney*, of *Norwich*, was seized the — of the Sixth Month 1772, with a Bleeding from the *Lungs*, which to her appeared likely to end her Days speedily. She laid quiet, and said calmly, *She had not any thing criminal in outward Things on her Mind, and she hoped in the Mercy of God.*

For many Weeks there seemed some flattering Symptoms, she said not much about them, but appear'd to be under a secret Exercise of Mind. As her Husband was sitting by her one Forenoon, she, in a very solid humble Frame of Spirit, spake to this Effect: *My dear, God is good indeed, a Father of tender Mercies. I feel his Mercy renewed to me. I shall die of this Ilness; but I shall be happy, and I am quite willing to go. When I was visited with the Truth, I had as it were an Offer made me of a rich Seat in the Kingdom of Heaven; but O the World has been too much for me! And many have been my bitter Baptisms for Disobedience; and yet, O thou merciful Father! thou hast forgiven me, and I shall have a Mansion with thee to Eternity.*

Many,

Many, very many, were the comfortable Expreffions that fhe utter'd upon various Occafions. One Evening on her Hufband taking leave of her, fhe faid fweetly, *I have an afflicted Body, but an eafy Mind* ; and fhe frequently expreft her perfect Refignation to her Heavenly Father's Will, who might juftly be faid to be long-fuffering and forbearing to her, tho' very unworthy ; but fhe had loved and ferved him in fome degree, and further faid, *If it was his Will to fpare her Life and to require it of her, fhe would acknowledge him in the Congregations of his People, or in any other Way he pleafed.*

When her three Brothers came from *London* to fee her, obferving one of them to be much tendered and affected, fhe defired, *They would not grieve for her but for themfelves, that they might experience the fame Comfort when the fame awful Vifitation might be theirs, as it certainly in a little Time would be* : Or to the fame Import.

The fecond Vifit her Father paid her in this Ilnefs, fhe expreft herfelf thus : *Dear Father, I have always loved thee, no Child could love a Parent more than I have loved thee* ; and after fome Paufe, *dear Father, I have been enabled to pray fervently to the Almighty for an eafy Paffage, and that I might have*

have a small Mansion in the Kingdom ; and, O Father ! there never can be a stronger Proof of the Holy Spirit, for the Answer was as if it was an outward Voice, Thou shalt enter into a full Fruition of Joy.

The Divine Mercy of God was indeed richly extended to her throughout her whole Ilness, and was her Stay and Support, by which, although her Sufferings were great, her Patience and Meekness were wonderful. Such a Calmness and Composure covered her Mind, that she disposed all her Affairs, and directed Things to be done after her Decease, without any visible Discomposure to herself. She lay many Weeks wishing for her Dissolution, and when she thought her Husband too anxious for her, she would say, *I desire thee not to grieve for me. It would be cruel to desire my Continuance in this Affliction, as all will be well with me.*

The last Day of her Life, as he was sitting by her as usual, she desired every Body to leave the Room but him and the young Woman that attended her ; and after a Pause of Quietness, she uttered such Expressions as these : *My Dear, it has for some Time been a close trying Season to me. Many deep Conflicts have I passed through, and that Heavenly Peace I felt in Weeks past has much left me ;* but

but yet I have a little Hope I shall have a Mansion in the Kingdom. In Reply to this State of deep Probation, her Husband spoke a little to her as Matter came before him, and she was very calm and humble, and after a considerable Time in Silence she called him again to her, and said, *How gracious and merciful is God! I think I now see the Seat I was first offered in my Heavenly Father's House, and I feel an Assurance I shall have it. This Affliction has been a great Refinement to my poor Mind. My Heavenly Father's Arms are open to receive me, and I die rejoicing.*

After this unutterable Favour she laid very quiet, and in Divine Sweetness fell into a Dose. When she awoke she expressed her Fears lest she should have a hard Passage, wishing it might be otherwise, and seemed revived. The Family were ordered to go to Bed (it being about Nine in the Evening) except a Friend and *Elizabeth Parkinson* the young Woman who waited on her, who, with her Husband sat quietly by her ; and about Ten o' Cock, without any visible Alteration to them, she departed, having had her Desire granted, and no doubt is entered into everlasting Felicity.

She

She died the 4th of the Tenth Month 1772, in the thirty-fifth Year of her Age, and was interred in Friends Burying-ground at *Norwich* the 11th Day of the same Month.

JOHN WOOLMAN, of the Province of *West-Jersey* in *America*, was born at *Northampton* in that Province, of Parents professing with Friends, who had a tender Care over him; and being good Examples themselves, promoted every Appearance of Good in him.

About the seventh Year of his Age, he became acquainted with the Operations of Divine Love in his Heart, and as he went from School one Seventh-day, whilst his Companions were at play he went forwards out of Sight, and setting himself down read the 22d Chapter of the *Revelations: He shewed me a River of Water, clear as Chrystal, proceeding out of the Throne of God and the Lamb,* &c. in reading of which, his Mind was drawn to seek after that pure Habitation which he then believed God had prepared for his Servants: The Place where he sat, and the Sweetness that attended his Mind, remained fresh in his Memory for many Years afterwards. This and the like

E e

gracious

gracious Vifitations had fuch an Effect upon him, that when he heard Boys make Ufe of ill Language it troubled him, and through the continued Mercies of God, he experienced Prefervation from it himfelf ; and the pious Inftruction of his Parents would recur frefh in his Mind when he happened to be among wicked Children, which was of Ufe to him. His Parents, who had a large Family of Children, frequently on the Firft-day of the Week after Meeting, employ'd them in reading the Scriptures or other good Books, one after the other, the reft fitting by for Inftruction.

In fome Memoirs left behind, he records this as a good Practice, and worthy of Imitation by thofe who are entrufted with the Care of Children. Thus in his very young Years, through the Renewings of Divine Love on his tender Mind, he was preferved from many Snares incident to Youth, until he had attain'd about the fixteenth Year of his Age, when as appears by his own Account, through Unwatchfulnefs he fuffered his Mind to be carried away by a Love of improper Company, and tho' preferved from profane Language or fcandalous Conduct, there was ftill a Plant alive which brought forth wild Grapes ; and though at Times he was brought ferioufly to confider

h. is

his Ways, which affected his Mind with Sorrow, yet by an Inattention to these Reproofs of Instruction, Vanity was added to Vanity, and Repentance to Repentance, and his Mind became alienated from the Truth and hasted towards Destruction; "Whilst," says he, in his Memoirs, "I meditate on the Gulf to-
" wards which I travelled, and reflect on my
" youthful Disobedience, mine Eyes run
" down with Water." Nevertheless, afterward his Mind became more estranged from the Enjoyment of real Good, and he ran greater Lengths in Vanity, until it pleased the Lord to visit him with Sickness, which appear'd to be nigh unto Death ; in which State, Darkness, Horror and Amazement seized his Mind, and he thought it would have been better for him never to have had a Being in this World, than to see such a Day of Confusion, and Affliction of Body and Mind ; herein he bewailed himself, and Cries ascended to an offended God, who in his Mercy at length heard him, and that Word which is as a Fire and a Hammer, broke and dissolved his rebellious Heart into a State of Contrition, which was succeeded with inward Consolation and Desires, *That if the Lord would be pleased to restore his Health, he might walk humbly before him.* And though the first Part of his Desire was granted, he again relapsed into Folly and Vanity ; of one

Instance

Inftance thereof take his own Account, *viz.*
" I remember once having fpent a Part of
" the Day in Wantonnefs, as I went to Bed
" at Night there lay in a Window near my
" Bed a Bible, which I opened and firft caft
" my Eye on the Text, *We lie down in our*
" *Shame and our Confufion covers us* ; this I
" knew to be my Cafe, and meeting with
" fo unexpected a Reproof, I was fomewhat
" affected by it, and went to Bed under
" Remorfe of Confcience, which I foon caft
" off again." But at length through the
powerful Operation of Divine Love, he was
enabled to take up the Crofs, and lived a
very retired religious Life, until it pleafed
the great Author of our Beings, about the
twenty-fecond Year of his Age, to commit
to him a Difpenfation of the Gofpel-Miniftry ;
and through Faithfulnefs thereto, he witneffed
an Increafe of thofe Talents committed to his
Care, and vifited moft of the *American* Provinces at different Times : And about the
Year 1763, during the *Indian* War, he
travelled about two Hundred Miles into the
back Parts of *Pennfilvania* (though attended
with great Fatigue of Body and Danger of
his Life) in order to pay a religious Vifit to
an *Indian* Settlement there, which was fa-
vourably received by the Natives, and doubt-
lefs was attended with Peace to his own Mind,
as he found many of them fufceptible of
                                            Divine

Divine Impreſſions. And alſo he was for many Years deeply exerciſed on Behalf of the poor enſlaved *Africans*, and both by Word and Writing, endeavour'd to convince Mankind of that unrighteous Traffick and Injuſtice of keeping them in Slavery.

In the Year 1772, with the Concurrence and Unity of his Brethren, he came over to this Nation to viſit Friends here, and landed in *London* about the 8th of the Sixth Month, and the Yearly-meeting being then ſitting, he attended that Meeting, in the Courſe of which he had to drop divers weighty and inſtructive Remarks ; but his Mind being drawn towards the North, he ſoon departed from this City, and by the Way of *Hertford*, *Buckinghamſhire*, *Northampton* and *Banbury* Quarterly-meetings, he proceeded to the Quarterly meeting at *York*, where after having attended moſt of the Sittings thereof, he was taken ill of the *Small Pox*, in which Diſorder he continued about two Weeks, at Times under great Affliction of Body, and then departed in full Aſſurance of a happy Eternity, as the following Expreſſions, amongſt others, taken from his own Mouth, do plainly evidence.

One Day being aſked how he felt himſelf, he meekly anſwered, *I don't know that I have ſlept flept this Night : I feel the Diforder making its Progrefs, but my Mind is mercifully pre-ferved in Stilnefs and Peace.* Some Time after he faid, *He was fenfible the Pains of Death muft be hard to bear, but if he efcaped them now, he muft fome Time pafs through them, and did not know he could be better prepared, but had no Will in it.* Said, *He had fettled his outward Affairs to his Mind; had taken leave of his Wife and Family, as never to return, leaving them to the Divine Protection;* adding, *and though I feel them near to me at this Time, yet I freely give them up, having an Hope they will be provided for.* And a little after faid, *This Trial is made eafier than I could have thought, by my Will being wholly taken away; for if I was anxious as to the Event, it would be harder, but I am not, and my Mind enjoys a perfect Calm.*

In the Night a young Woman having given him fomething to drink, he faid, *My Child, thou feemeft very kind to me, a poor Creature, the Lord will reward thee for it.* A while after he cried out with great Ear-neftnefs of Spirit, *O my Father! my Father! how comfortable art thou to my Soul in this trying Seafon.* Being afked if he could take a little Nourifhment, after fome Paufe he replied, *My Child, I cannot tell what to fay*
to

*to it ; I seem nearly arrived where my Soul
shall have Rest from all its Troubles.* After
giving in something to be put into his Journal, he said, *I believe the Lord will now
excuse me from Exercises of this Kind, and I
see no Work but one, which is to be the last
wrought by me in this World ; the Messenger
will come that will release me from all these
Troubles, but it must be in the Lord's Time,
which I am waiting for.* He said, *He had
laboured to do whatever was required, according to the Ability received, in the Remembrance
of which he had Peace. And though the
Disorder was strong at Times, and would
come over his Mind like a Whirlwind, yet it
had hitherto been kept steady, and center'd in
everlasting Love ;* adding, *and if that's mercifully continued, I ask nor desire no more.*

At another Time he said, *He had long
had a View of visiting this Nation ; and some
Time before he came, he had a Dream, in
which he saw himself in the Northern Parts of
it ; and that the Spring of the Gospel was
opened in him, much as in the Beginning of
Friends, such as* George Fox *and* William
Dewsbury ; *and he saw the different States of
People as clear as ever he had seen Flowers
in a Garden ; but in his going on he was
suddenly stopt, though he could not see for
what End, but looked towards Home, and in*
that

that fell into a Flood of Tears, which waked him.

At another Time he said, *My Draught seem'd strongest to the North, and I mentioned in my own Monthly-meeting, that attending the Quarterly-meeting at York, and being there, looked like Home to me.*

Having repeatedly confented to take a Medicine with a View to fettle his Stomach, but without Effect, the Friend then waiting on him, faid, through Diftrefs, What fhall I do now? He anfwered with great Compofure, *Rejoice evermore, and in every Thing give Thanks:* But added a little after, *This is fometimes hard to come at.*

One Morning early he brake forth in Supplication on this wife: *O Lord! it was thy Power that enabled me to forfake Sin in my Youth, and I have felt thy Bruifes fince for Difobedience, but as I bowed under them thou healedft me; and though I have gone through many Trials and fore Afflictions, thou haft been with me, continuing a Father and a Friend: I feel thy Power now, and beg that in the approaching trying Moments, thou wilt keep my Heart ftedfaft unto thee.* Upon his giving the fame Friend Directions concerning fome little Matters, fhe faid, I will take Care,

Care, but hope thou mayft live to order them thyfelf; he replied, *My Hope is in Chrift; and though I may now feem a little better, a Change in the Diforder may foon happen, and my little Strength be diffolved, and if it fo happen, I fhall be gather'd to my everlafting Reft.* On her faying, She did not doubt that, but could not help mourning to fee fo many faithful Servants removed at fo low a Time; he faid, *All Goodnefs cometh from the Lord, whofe Power is the fame, and he can work as he fees beft.* The fame Day, after giving her Directions about wrapping his Corps, and perceiving her to weep, he faid, *I had rather thou wouldft guard againft Weeping or Sorrowing for me, my Sifter; I forrow not, though I have had fome painful Conflicts; but now they feem over, and Matters all fettled; and I look at the Face of my dear Redeemer, for fweet is his Voice, and his Countenance comely.*

Being very weak, and in general difficult to be underftood, he uttered a few Words in Commemoration of the Lord's Goodnefs to him; and added, *How tenderly have I been waited upon in this Time of Affliction, in which I may fay in* Job's *Words, Tedious Days and wearifome Nights are appointed unto me; and how many are fpending their Time and Money in Vanity and Superfluities, while*

F f

Thousands and Tens of Thousands want the Necessaries of Life, who might be relieved by them, and their Distresses at such a Time as this, in some degree softened by the administring of suitable Things.

An Apothecary who attended him of his own Accord (he being unwilling to have any sent for) appeared very anxious to assist him, with whom conversing, he queried about the Probability of such a Load of Matter being thrown off his weak Body, and the Apothecary making some Remarks, implying he thought it might, he spoke with an audible Voice on this wise: *My Dependance is in the Lord Jesus Christ, who I trust will forgive my Sins, which is all I hope for ; and if it be his Will to raise up this Body again, I am content, and if to die I am resigned: And if thou canst not be easy without trying to assist Nature, in order to lengthen out my Life, I submit.* After this, his Throat was so much affected, that it was very difficult for him to speak so as to be understood, and he frequently wrote when he wanted any thing. About the second Hour on Fourth-day Morning, being the 7th of the Tenth Month, 1772, he asked for Pen and Ink, and at several Times, with much Difficulty, wrote thus : " I believe my being here is in " the Wisdom of Christ ; I know not as to

" Life

"Life or Death." About a Quarter before Six the same Morning, he seemed to fall into an easy Sleep, which continued about half an Hour, when seeming to awake, he breathed a few Times with more Difficulty, and so expired without Sigh, Groan, or Struggle.

Note, He often said, *It was hid from him, whether he might recover, or not, and he was not desirous to know it ; but from his own Feeling of the Disorder, and his feeble Constitution, thought he should not.*

WILLIAM YOUNG, Son of *William Young*, of *Leominster* in the County of *Hereford*, and *Hannah* his Wife, she being deceased, was in his Childhood of a sweet and sprightly natural Temper, and altho' of a tender Frame, seemed healthy, until he contracted a Cold, which at length brought on a *Consumption*.

In the Course of his Affliction his Deportment was grave, and as he grew worse, he became more thoughtful, and made many sensible Remarks of the Uncertainty of visible Things ; and expressed a grateful Sense of the Kindness of Providence many Ways,

and

and particularly in the Visits and good Advice he received from Friends; for although he had been preserved in a more innocent Conduct than most young Men of his Age, he knew that would not intitle him to the Felicity of the Redeemed, and was therefore earnestly desirous of attaining such a State of inward Purity and Renovation of Heart as would procure Divine Favour; and on this Account had many painful Conflicts: And when his Recovery was thought doubtful, often lamented his having lost that Tenderness and Fervency of Spirit towards God which he had formerly experienced.

For many Weeks before his Death he was apprehensive of his End being near, and said, *If I die now in my Youth, it may be all for the best, and may put other young People upon the Consideration of their Latter-end*; and on his Father's saying, It would be well for us to be resigned to the Divine Will, but intimating a Reluctancy to part, he replied with much Earnestness, *Aye, do be resigned, let us all be resigned*; and frequently expressed a Desire to be resigned either to Life or Death; but said, *If it pleased the Lord to fit him for his Change, and take him from the slippery Paths of Life at so early a Period, he should think it a Favour; for he had no Desire to live except it was to the Glory of his Creator.*

He

He several Times shewed great Concern at hearing of the disorderly Walking of some amongst us, and a deep Sense of the wonderful Goodness and Condescention of Christ in suffering for Mankind.

Some Weeks before his Death, observing his Sister weep, he said, *We must part, I must leave you ; but I hope and believe we shall meet again.*

The 2d of the First Month he was very ill, and seeing his Father affected, he said, *O Father, what a Mercy it will be if the Lord should be pleased to take me to himself ! Do not grieve, for if I should be spared and turn out naught, it would be a greater Affliction.*

The next Morning, after having had a very bad Night, he was weak and low, but appeared quite calm in Mind ; and on his Sister's saying after some other Conversation, She hoped he was resigned ; he replied with much Sweetness, *Yes Sister, I hope I am quite resigned to the Almighty's Will ; but surely if it is his Will, it will be a Mercy to be taken from this troublesome World to himself ; and I have a Hope he will take me to himself, he hath been pleased wonderfully to calm my Mind.* She observed, There was great Room to

hope,

hope, and that the Sufferings of his Friends
would be greateft ; he replied very earneftly,
*O my Sufferings will be nothing in Proportion
to my Offences ! but I have a Hope my Offences will be forgiven. O how merciful is
the Lord ! How great is his Goodnefs ! How
pure is his Love ! Mercy, Goodnefs, Purity,
belong to him.* After feeing his Sifter much
affected at what he faid, he continued, *We
cannot tell Sifter, fome worfe than me have
been reftored, he is able to raife me up, and
if he fhould, and make me fome Sort of a
Member* (meaning of his Church Militant)
*I hope I fhall be careful to keep near to him ;
but I defire not to live, no not a Moment, as
one of this World.*

That Night he was fo weak thofe about
him were apprehenfive he could not continue
long ; the next Day he feemed pretty free
from Pain, but drowfy, and his Expreffions
rambling, but quite innocent ; indeed his
Countenance and Converfation was fweet and
lamb-like. The next Morning he defired to
be put to Bed, being in great Pain, but
could not reft there ; and being replaced in
the eafy Chair and fame Pofture he had lain
for many Nights, feemed much eafier, and
told his Sifter, *He was going ;* fhe faid, She
hoped to a better Inheritance, he replied,
Aye, for I believe in one that can fave me ;
and

and repeatedly faid, *The Fear of Death was taken away.* And a Day or two before his Death, he faid, *I am going to leave an affectionate Father to meet the great Almighty Father.*

Another Time, his Sifter faying, It was a Favour he was preferved fo patient, he faid, *I hope I fhall be kept fo, I am under the Lord's Care intirely ; nothing elfe will do, I fee nothing elfe will do.* The fame Day he uttered many fweet and lively Expreffions, but his Voice was too low to be underftood, fo as to connect the Sentences ; and the Day before his Deceafe, it was fo weak and broken, that he could fcarcely articulate a Sentence ; but was meek and patient as a Lamb, and once faid fomething about rejoicing in the Houfe of God, and when he could no otherwife exprefs himfelf, would reach up to kifs his Father and Sifter, his Heart being full of Love ; when afked, If he would have any thing to his eldeft Sifter then in Cornwall ? He faid, *Nothing but my Love, or dear Love ;* adding, *In that Love I feel for all.* He frequently defired them about him not to grieve, and would fometimes fay, *Why, if you think I am going well, fhould you grieve ;* and obferved, *That if he had brought on his Illnefs by any bad Courfe of Life, it would be hard to bear ;* but, added, *I believe*

I believe have no Reaſon to think I have.
He took a moſt affectionate leave of his
Siſter, bidding her, *Love and adore the Lord;*
and ſaid ſomething about his Father, which
could not be underſtood; his Father then
telling him, He hoped there was a Place
prepared for him amongſt the Bleſſed, and
that he loved to be with the Good, he
replied as well as he was able, *Aye, dearly,
dearly.* And in about two Hours after,
departed ſo quietly that thoſe preſent apprehended him fallen aſleep, on the 7th Day
of the Firſt Month 1773, in the nineteenth
Year of his Age.

HANNAH DUDLEY, late
Wife of *Robert Dudley,* of *Clonmell*
in *Ireland,* was born at *Woodbridge* in *Suffolk,*
and religiouſly educated, which was bleſſed
to her; and through the prevailing Power
of Divine Love, ſhe was brought to know
a State of Submiſſion to divers near Trials
which fell to her Lot; and having her
Heart wean'd from the World and its deluſive Profits and Friendſhips, ſhe became
more and more refined, being an Example
of Humility, Plainneſs and Self-denial.

About

About the Year 1772 fome Symptoms of a *Confumption* appear'd, but for fome Time fhe attended Meetings, both for Worfhip and Difcipline, in fome of which fhe was enabled to bear a living Teftimony to the Truth.

In the Courfe of her Ilnefs many Friends vifited her, to whom fhe was enabled to drop fome tender Expreffions, and it feemed to be her greateft Joy to fee and hear of the Profperity of Truth; and at divers Opportunities fhe had fuitable Counfel and Inftruction to give to thofe about her.

About a Week before her Departure, our Friend *Robert Willis,* of *Weft-Jerfey* in *America*, being in the Courfe of his religious Vifit at her Houfe, had a comfortable and tendering Opportunity with her, her Hufband and Sifter.

About two Days before her Deceafe, fhe dropt much excellent Counfel and Advice to her Hufband and Sifter, expreffing, *Her Defire to be releafed*; but added, *Her Hope fhe fhould be preferved patient to the End*; and afterwards on fome Mitigation of her Pain, fignified, *Her intire Refignation to the Divine Will*; and fpeaking to her Hufband's eldeft Son, in a very weighty Manner ad-

vifed

vised him, *To remember her Admonitions;* saying also, *Shun bad Company, obey thy Parent, and do not offend him; seek the Lord and he will be found of thee, but if thou forsake him he will cast thee off for ever.*

To their Apprentice, she said, *Jemmy, love Plainness and continue in it, for Truth leads to Plainness; thou hast been favour'd with an Education beyond many, therefore prize it, and hast known Truth, therefore beware of trampling on the Testimony, but be circumspect in all thy Ways and Conduct; thou art just entering on the slippery Part of Life, the slippery Paths of Youth, and art no Stranger to the Temptations and Allurements of the Adversary: I have often thought it a great Mercy, that thou hast been preserved from (I believe) almost any Vice.* Just after, she very affectionately took her leave of her Brother and Sister-in-Law, saying, *Our Acquaintance has been short, but we have loved one another;* and then prayed very fervently that a Blessing might rest upon their Family.

Being pressed to try and take a little Sleep, she replied, *O that I could sleep in the Arms of my Beloved!* And with great Fervency prayed, *O Lord God have Mercy upon me! and let thy compassionate Ear be opened. Lord God*

God Almighty! send the guardian Angel of thy Presence to conduct my Spirit. After which she lay in great Peace and Serenity of Mind, growing weaker and weaker, yet sensible to the last, and with her Hand closed in her Husband's, departed without Sigh or Groan, as one falling into a sweet Sleep, the 25th of the First Month 1773. Aged about forty-seven Years, a Minister about nine Years. After a very large and solemn Meeting her Body was decently interred, the 29th, in Friends Burial-ground in *Clonmell* aforesaid.

SAMUEL FOTHERGILL, of *Warrington* in *Lancashire*, was the sixth Son of our worthy ancient Friend *John Fothergill*, mentioned in this Treatise, see Page 29, and of *Margaret* his Wife, for an Account of whom see Volume the sixth, Page 90, of *Piety Promoted*.

This their Son being of an active and lively Disposition, and during his Apprenticeship mostly from under the watchful Eye of his affectionate Parent, he fled from the Holy Cross of Christ, and indulged himself in the Gratifications of Folly and Licentiousness, violating the repeated Convictions of Divine Grace in his own Mind, which had

G g 2

been

been mercifully extended from his early
Years, thereby wounding the Soul of his
tender Father (of whose religious Care to
form and lead the tender Minds of his Children to Piety and Virtue we have an Account
in the Memoirs of his Life;) yet his pious
Admonitions proved nevertheless, as Bread
cast on the Waters, which return'd after many
Days; for about the twenty-first Year of his
Age, the Visitation of Divine Love was so
powerfully renewed, that it proved effectual
to turn his Steps out of the Paths of Vanity;
and as he has expressed, with humble and
awful Gratitude to the Preserver of Men, *It
then appeared clear to his Understanding, that
would be the last Call the Heavenly Father
would favour him with*; he therefore consulted no longer with Flesh and Blood, but
gave up to the Holy Visitation, devoting his
whole Heart and Affections to seek Recon-
ciliation with God, through the Mediation
of Jesus Christ; and abiding in great Humility under the purifying Operation of the
Holy Ghost and Fire, he became thereby
qualified for those eminent Services he was
called into; for in a few Months, by the
constraining Power and Love of God, his
Mouth was opened to bear a Testimony to
the Sufficiency of that Holy Arm that had
plucked him as a Brand out of the Fire:
Thus a Dispensation of the Ministry being
committed

committed to his Charge, he attended faithfully thereto, and moved therein at the Requirings, and under the Direction of Divine Wifdom, by which Means he foon became an able Minifter of the Gofpel, called thereto and qualified by the Holy Ghoft ; under which Influence he laboured with Diligence, and devoted much of his Time and Strength, when Health permitted, to the Service of his dear Lord and Mafter ; for the Continuance of whofe Favours he counted nothing too near or dear to part with, that he might be inftrumental in gathering Souls to God, which was the Object he had in View in all his Gofpel-Labours ; being diligent himfelf, he endeavoured much to excite Friends to a due and conftant Attendance of Meetings for religious Worfhip, and thofe for the Difcipline of the Church.

Thro' the Courfe of his Gofpel-Labours, both in Publick and Private, animated by Divine Love, he exprefled an uncommon Warmth of Affection for the rifing Youth of this Generation, with whom he was frequently led into a deep brotherly Feeling and Sympathy for their prefent and eternal Welfare ; under which Concern his Love to this Clafs of both Sexes, under all Denominations, was ftrong and ardent.

He

He travelled much in this Nation and *Scotland*, several Times in *Ireland*, and once through most of the *North-American* Colonies, in the Service of Truth ; where, tho' singularly humbled in a Sense of Poverty, Weakness and Insufficiency on his first landing, he was by Accounts received, marveloufly strengthened, both in Public and Private, in Gofpel-Authority and Love, to the awakening and comforting of many.

In the fore Part of the Year 1769, he visited most of the Families of Friends in the Monthly-meeting of *Grace-church-street, London* ; in which Service he was divinely strengthened and enabled to extend a helping Hand to many in close and necessary Labour, for their increasing Care, to live and act consistent with our Holy Profession, to the Comfort and Help of divers, and his own Peace ; and afterwards, at two different Opportunities, he visited the Families of Friends in *Horflydown* and *Westminster* Monthly-meetings in that City, to the same good Effect.

He mostly attended the Yearly-meetings in *London*, and other Places, when of bodily Ability ; in which his Gofpel-Labours were very acceptable and edifying ; being particularly careful when called from Home, to return to his Family and Friends with as much

much Expedition as the Nature of his Service would admit.

Having acquired a moderate Competency by his Diligence and Induſtry, he declined Trade for ſeveral Years before his Deceaſe, devoting his Time and Talents to the Service of the Churches. As a Pillar in the Lord's Houſe he was ſtedfaſt, being actuated by a *Chriſtian* and manly Zeal ; in Deportment grave ; his private Converſation was ſavory and edifying, correſponding with his Miniſtry, which at Times went forth as a Flame, piercing the Obdurate, yet deſcended like Dew upon the tender Plants of our Heavenly Father's planting, the true Mourners in Zion, with theſe he travelled in a deep Sympathy of Spirit ; in his Goſpel-Labours free from Affectation, in Doctrine clear, ſound and pathetic, filled with Charity, allowing for the Prejudices of Mankind, being indeed a Miniſter and Elder worthy of double Honour, ſpeaking whereof he knew, and what his own Hands had handled of the good Word of Life.

He endured a long and painful Ilneſs with much Patience and Reſignation, and towards the Cloſe of his Time expreſſed himſelf to ſome of his Relations, when they took leave of him, previous to their ſetting out for the
Yearly-

Yearly-meeting in *London*, to the following Effect :

Our Health is no more at our Command, than Length of Days :——Mine seems drawing fast towards a Conclusion ;——but I am content with every Allotment of Providence, for they are all in Wisdom,—unerring Wisdom.

There is ONE THING *which as an Arm underneath, bears up and supports ; and tho' the rolling tempestuous Billows surround, yet my Head is kept above them, and my Feet are firmly established.——O ! seek it,—press after it,—lay fast Hold of it.*

Tho' painful my Nights, and wearisome my Days, yet I am preserved in Patience and Resignation.——Death has no Terrors, nor will the Grave have any Victory.——My Soul triumphs over Death, Hell and the Grave.

Husbands and Wives, Parents and Children, Health and Riches, must all go.——Disappointment is another Name for them.

I should have been thankful had I been able to have got to the ensuing Yearly-meeting in London, *which you are now going to attend, where I have been so often refreshed with my Brethren ; but it is otherwise allotted.——I*

shall

shall remember them, and some of them will remember me.——The Lord knows best what is best for us; I am content and resigned to his Will.

I feel a Foretaste of that Joy that is to come;—— and who would wish to change such a State of Mind?

I should be glad if an easy Channel could be found to inform the Yearly-meeting, that as I have lived, so I shall close, with the most unshaken Assurance, that we have not followed cunningly devised Fables, but the pure, living eternal Substance.

Let the Aged be strong, let the Middle-aged be animated, and the Youth encouraged; for the Lord is still with Sion; the Lord will bless Sion.

If I be now removed out of his Church Militant, where I have endeavoured in some Measure to fill up my Duty, I have an EVIDENCE *that I shall gain an Admittance into his glorious Church Triumphant, far above the Heavens.*

My dear Love is to all them that love the Lord Jesus.

H h   He

He departed this Life at his Houſe in *Warrington* the 15th, and was buried the 19th Day of the Sixth Month 1772, at *Penheth,* in the fifty-ſeventh Year of his Age, and the thirty-ſixth of his Miniſtry.

AND now, READER, before thou cloſe the Book, pauſe a little, conſider, what Progreſs thou has made in this Heavenly Race. The Prophet *Iſaiah,* after deſcribing the Coming of Chriſt, and very emphatically ſetting forth his Office, the peaceable Government of his Power, and its glorious Effects upon his Followers, in Chap. xi. in the next Chapter declares what the Faithful experience: *And in that Day thou ſhalt ſay, O Lord! I will praiſe thee; tho' thou was angry with me, thine Anger is turned away, and thou comfortedſt me. Behold, God is my Salvation, I will truſt and not be afraid; for the Lord Jehovah is my Strength, and my Song, he alſo is become my Salvation,* Iſaiah xii. 1, 2.

The ſame living Divine Power, the ſame inexhauſtible Source of Wiſdom and Goodneſs remains. The Enjoyments of Time are tranſient, its Pleaſures are deluſive; let therefore all truſt in his Arm, this is the Strength and

and Beauty of Men ; their alone Help and Dependance is here, in all their Exercises through Time, that when they come to close, as has been the Case with the Just in all Generations, in Effect, to declare, *Behold God is my Salvation, I will trust and not be afraid ; for the Lord Jehovah is my Strength and my Song, he also is become my Salvation.*

A N

AN INDEX

OF THE

Perſons NAMES

Contained in this VOLUME.

The INDEX.

The INDEX.

The INDEX.

FINIS.